*"You know about all this family stuff. You're compassionate. You're a woman."*

If Grace had been on her feet, she'd probably have fainted at the admission. "That has to be a first," she commented.

"What?" Michael asked.

"You admitting you're at a loss."

He regarded her evenly. "I'm not blind to my faults, Grace."

"Just not interested in correcting them?" she surmised.

His gaze narrowed. "Do you really want to take that particular walk down memory lane?"

Her cheeks burned. She swallowed hard and shook her head, reminding herself that his calling her wasn't personal. He hadn't dragged her over here because he'd been pining away for her for the past few years. It was about those two scared boys upstairs. Nothing else. Period. She had to keep that in mind. It would be way too easy to get caught up in all of this, to imagine that they were partners, a team, a family....

Dear Reader,

As the beautiful fall foliage, sweet apple cider and crisp air beckon you outside, Silhouette Special Edition ushers you back *inside* to savor six exciting, brand-new romances!

Watch for *Bachelor's Baby Promise* by Barbara McMahon—October's tender THAT'S MY BABY! title—which features a tall, dark and handsome bachelor who takes on fatherhood—and the woman of his dreams! And romance unfolds in *Marrying a Delacourt* as bestselling author Sherryl Woods delivers another exciting installment in her wildly popular AND BABY MAKES THREE: THE DELACOURTS OF TEXAS miniseries. Sparks fly when a charming rogue claims the wrong bride in *Millionaire Takes a Bride* by Pamela Toth, the first book in HERE COME THE BRIDES—a captivating new trilogy about beautiful triplet sisters by three of your favorite authors. Look for the second installment next month!

One tiny baby draws two former lovers back together again in *A Bundle of Miracles* by Amy Frazier, who pays tribute to National Breast Cancer Awareness Month with this heartwrenching novel. Fierce passion flares in *Hidden in a Heartbeat* by Patricia McLinn, the third book in her A PLACE CALLED HOME miniseries. And not to be missed, talented new author Ann Roth unravels a soul-searing tale about a struggling single mom and a brooding stranger in *Stranger in a Small Town*.

I hope you enjoy all of our books this month as Special Edition continues to celebrate Silhouette's 20th anniversary!

All the best,

Karen Taylor Richman
Senior Editor

Please address questions and book requests to:
Silhouette Reader Service
U.S.: 3010 Walden Ave., P.O. Box 1325, Buffalo, NY 14269
Canadian: P.O. Box 609, Fort Erie, Ont. L2A 5X3

# SHERRYL WOODS

## MARRYING A DELACOURT

# SPECIAL EDITION®

Published by Silhouette Books

**America's Publisher of Contemporary Romance**

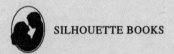 SILHOUETTE BOOKS

ISBN 0-373-24352-9

MARRYING A DELACOURT

Visit Silhouette at www.eHarlequin.com

Printed in U.S.A.

# SHERRYL WOODS

Whether she's living in California, Florida or Virginia, Sherryl Woods always makes her home by the sea. A walk on the beach, the sound of waves, the smell of the salt air all provide inspiration for this writer of more than sixty romance and mystery novels. Sherryl hopes you're enjoying these latest entries in the AND BABY MAKES THREE series for Silhouette Special Edition. You can write to Sherryl or—from April through December—stop by and meet her at her bookstore, Potomac Sunrise, 308 Washington Avenue, Colonial Beach, VA 22443.

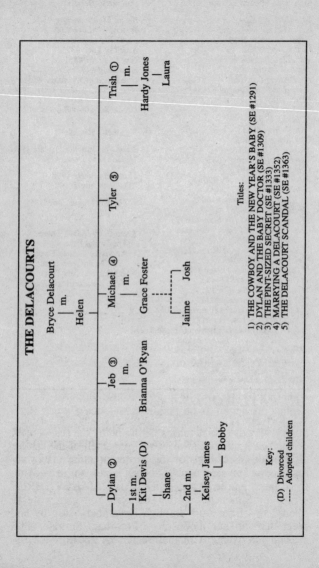

# THE DELACOURTS

Bryce Delacourt
m.
Helen

Dylan ② — Jeb ③ — Michael ④ — Tyler ⑤ — Trish ①

**Dylan ②**
1st m.
Kit Davis (D)
— Shane
2nd m.
Kelsey James
└ Bobby

**Jeb ③**
m.
Brianna O'Ryan

**Michael ④**
m.
Grace Foster
┌─────┴─────┐
Jaime      Josh

**Trish ①**
m.
Hardy Jones
Laura

Titles:

1) THE COWBOY AND THE NEW YEAR'S BABY (SE #1291)
2) DYLAN AND THE BABY DOCTOR (SE #1309)
3) THE PINT-SIZED SECRET (SE #1333)
4) MARRYING A DELACOURT (SE #1352)
5) THE DELACOURT SCANDAL (SE #1363)

Key:
(D) Divorced
---- Adopted children

# Chapter One

If Michael Delacourt had had any idea that this latest harangue about his health was going to bring the bane of his existence, Grace Foster, back into his life, he would have tuned Tyler out. Instead, he let his brother drone on and on, then fell right straight into the trap.

"You're a heart attack waiting to happen," Tyler Delacourt began as he had at least once a week like clockwork. He made the claim with brotherly concern, usually from the comfortable vantage point of the sofa in Michael's office on the executive floor at Delacourt Oil. He was slugging down black coffee and doughnuts as he spoke, unaware of the irony in his comments. "You have to learn how to slow down—before it's too late."

*Too late? Hogwash!* Michael was getting sick of

hearing it, especially from a man who shunned exercise unless it was related to bringing in a new gusher. Worse, Tyler's consumption of cholesterol showed a total disregard for its potential effects on *his* heart.

Besides, Michael thought irritably, he wasn't even in his thirties yet. Okay, he was close, weeks away, in fact. Still, by all accounts this was the prime of his life. Just as he was doing this morning, he did thirty grueling minutes every day on the treadmill he kept in his office. Hell, he was in better shape now than he'd been in when he'd played college sports. Could Tyler say the same?

"I'd like to see you set the pace I do on this treadmill," he countered as sweat poured down his chest and his muscles burned from the exertion.

But even as he dismissed his brother's concern, Michael was forced to admit that he exercised the way he did everything else—as if driven. His bewildered mother used to say he'd come out of the womb three weeks early, and he'd been in a hurry ever since. It was a trait that definitely set him apart from his laid-back brothers—Dylan, Jeb and, especially, Tyler. Michael was not prone to a lot of introspection, but he could hardly deny that his type-A personality affected all aspects of his life, personal as well as professional.

To top it off, he had no social life to speak of, unless his command attendance at various benefits and dinner parties counted. He was as wary of females as a man could get. The minute a woman started making possessive little remarks, he beat a hasty retreat. Maybe someday, when he had some spare time, he'd sit down and try to figure out why. In the meantime, he simply accepted the fact that there was no room in his life for a woman who'd have to take second place to his career at Delacourt Oil.

Of the four Delacourt brothers, he was the only one who really gave a damn about the family business. He had his father's instincts for it. He had the drive and ambition to take the company to new heights, but Bryce Delacourt was fiercely determined that the company he'd launched would be divided equally among his offspring. He grumbled unrelentingly about how ungrateful they were for not seeing that, never noticing that Michael was grateful enough for all of them.

Still, Delacourt Oil was his father's baby, which he could split up any way he wanted to. It wasn't that Michael was unwilling to share with his siblings. It was just that he wanted to be the one on top, the one in charge, and he would run himself into the ground if necessary trying to prove that he was worthy of the position. None of the others understood that kind of single-minded determination. Even now, Tyler was shaking his head, disapproval written all over his face.

"That's just it. You exercise all out, as if you're trying to conquer Mount Everest, the same way you do everything," Tyler chided, refusing to let the subject drop. "You keep that blasted phone in your hand the whole time, too, so you're not wasting time."

"It's efficient," Michael said, defending himself for perhaps the thousandth time. He tossed his portable phone on the sofa next to Tyler to prove he could give it up any time he wanted to.

"It's crazy," Tyler contradicted. "Face it, you're a compulsive overachiever. Always have been. When was the last time you took a day off? When was the last time you took an actual vacation?"

"To do what?" Michael asked, perplexed.

"Go to the beach house with the rest of us, for instance. We haven't had a decent bachelor weekend in a couple of years now."

"Dylan and Jeb are married. I doubt their wives would approve of the sort of weekends we used to have over there," Michael said wryly.

Tyler grinned. "Probably not. Okay, so the wild bachelor days are over for poor Dylan and poor Jeb. That doesn't mean you and I can't spend a few days catching rays and chasing women. How about it? A week of sun and fun."

Michael was tempted. Then he thought of his jam-packed schedule. "I don't think so. Not any time soon, anyway. My calendar's booked solid."

"You *are* turning into a pitiful stick in the mud," his brother declared sorrowfully. "If you won't do that, how about going over to Los Piños for a few days to visit Trish and Dylan and their families? Spend a little quality time with our niece and nephew. Trish was saying just the other day that a visit is long overdue."

Guilt nagged at Michael for about ten seconds. "Yeah, well, I've been meaning to get over there, but you know how it is," he hedged.

"I know exactly how it is. Your niece is going on three years old and you haven't seen her since she was baptized when she was a month old. When Dylan and Kelsey got married, you barely stuck your head in the church over there long enough to hear their *I do's* before you took off for some can't-miss conference.''

"I was speaking at an OPEC meeting. Are you saying I should have turned down that chance?''

Tyler waved off the defense. ''I'll give you that one. But if it hadn't been OPEC, it would have been something else. What exactly are you afraid will happen if you take some time off? Do you think the rest of us are going to steal the company out from under you?''

He peered at Michael intently. ''You do realize what a joke that is, don't you? Trish wants no part of the business. She's happy as a clam running her bookstore and devoting her spare time to her husband and daughter. Dylan is perfectly content playing Dick Tracy across the state. Jeb is doing in-house security and wallowing in family life.''

"That still leaves you,'' Michael pointed out, aware that he was grasping at straws.

Tyler laughed. ''You know perfectly well that I'm trying my best to convince Dad to let me stay out in the field, exploring for oil. I'm heading back out onto one of our rigs in the Gulf of Mexico in another couple of weeks. I miss it. I miss Baton Rouge.''

Michael studied him. ''Who's in Baton Rouge, little brother?''

"I didn't say anything about a person. I mentioned an oil rig and a city.''

"But I know you. There has to be a woman involved.''

Tyler scowled. "We were talking about me competing for your job. It's not going to happen, Michael. Not only do I love what I do, it keeps me out from under Dad's thumb. Face it, none of your siblings wants a desk job here, thank you very much. It's all yours, big brother. There is no competition. This office in the executive suite is yours for life—if you want it."

Michael inwardly admitted that everything Tyler had just said was true. But that knowledge didn't keep him from working compulsively. "I love what I do, so shoot me," he muttered.

"You need a life," Tyler retorted. "You might think it's enough to be at the top of the list of Houston's most eligible bachelors, but you're going to look mighty funny if you're still there when you hit ninety."

"Why worry about my social life? A minute ago you claimed I'm destined to die of a heart attack before I turn forty. If that's the case, there's no point in leaving behind a wealthy widow."

Tyler waved off the attempt to divert him. "You're missing my point."

"Which is?"

"You need some balance in your life, Michael. Believe it or not, I actually recall a time when you were fun to be around, when you talked about something besides mergers and the price of crude oil."

Michael uttered a resigned sigh. Clearly, his brother was on a mission. Tyler was usually a live-and-let-live kind of a guy, but periodically he turned into a nag. This kind of persistence could only mean that he'd been put up to it by the rest of the family.

The one way to shut him up was to make a few well-intentioned promises.

"Okay, okay, I'll try to get a break in my schedule," Michael promised.

Tyler looked skeptical. "Not good enough. When?"

"Soon."

He shook his head, obviously not pacified by such a vague response. "Trish says her guest room is ready now," he said. "You can see your niece. You can see Dylan and his family. I'll even ride over with you on the company jet. We'll have ourselves an old-fashioned reunion."

Michael wasn't fooled for a minute. Tyler wasn't going on this proposed jaunt out of any great desire to hold a family barbecue. He'd been assigned to deliver his big brother into the protective arms of their baby sister.

Michael shuddered at the memory of the last time they'd all ganged up on him like this. He'd wound up in a deserted cabin in the woods for a solid week with no car and no phone. Instead of relaxing him, the forced solitude had almost driven him up a wall. He hadn't been able to convince his siblings that they hadn't done him any favors. A two-day visit with Trish's family would be heaven by comparison. He was smart enough to accept it while he still had a choice in the matter. His family wasn't above kidnapping him, and he doubted a court in the land would convict them for it once they made a convincing case that they'd done it for his own good.

"Set it up," he said, resigned to the inevitable. "Just let me know the details."

"We're leaving in fifteen minutes," Tyler announced, his expression instantly triumphant.

"But I can't—"

"Of course, you can," Tyler said, cutting off the protest. "Hop in the shower, get into your clothes and let's go. I have your suitcase at the airport and the pilot's on standby. Your secretary's canceled all your appointments for the next week."

"A week?" Michael protested. "I agreed to a couple of days."

"Your secretary must have misunderstood me," Tyler said with no evidence of remorse. "You know how she is."

"She's incredibly efficient, and I *thought* she was loyal to me."

"She is. That's why she wiped the slate clean for the next week. So you'll be able to take a long overdue break. You're free and clear, bro."

Michael frowned at Tyler. "Awfully damned sure of yourself, weren't you?"

"What can I say? I'm a born negotiator. It runs in the family. Now, hop to it."

Not until twenty-four hours later did Michael realize the full extent of his brother's treachery, when he found himself shut away on Trish's ranch, abandoned by his sister, her husband and the very niece he'd supposedly come to see.

Tyler had long since departed, claiming urgent business elsewhere. Probably a woman. That one he'd denied existed over in Baton Rouge. With Ty, it was always about a woman.

At any rate, one minute Michael had been sitting

at Trish's kitchen table surrounded by family, the next he'd been all alone and cursing the fact that he hadn't been an only child.

"It's Hardy's family," Trish had explained apologetically as she sashayed past him with little more than a perfunctory kiss on his cheek. "An emergency. We absolutely have to go. We shouldn't be gone more than a day or two."

Since the phone hadn't rung, he had to assume this crisis had occurred before his arrival. Naturally no one had thought for a second to simply call him and tell him to stay home.

"I hate doing this to you," his sister claimed, though she looked suspiciously cheerful. "The cattle shouldn't be any problem. Hardy's got that covered. You don't mind staying here and keeping an eye on the horses, though, do you? Somebody will be by to see that they're fed and let out into the corral, but you might want to exercise them."

Already reeling, at that point Michael had stared at his baby sister as if she'd lost her mind. "Trish, unless it has four wheels, I don't ride it."

"Of course you do."

"I was on a pony once when I was six. I fell off. All advice to the contrary, I did not get back on."

"Well, you're a Texan, aren't you? You'll get the knack of it while you're here," she'd said blithely. "We'll get back as soon as we can. Whatever you do, don't leave. I won't have your vacation ruined because of us. This is a great place to relax. Lots of peace and quiet. Make yourself right at home, okay? Love you."

And then she was gone. Michael felt as if he'd

been caught up in a tornado and dropped down again, dazed and totally lost. He knew he should have protested, told his sister that he'd be on his way first thing in the morning, but she already had one foot out the door when she asked him to stick around. She made this sudden trip sound like a blasted emergency. She made it seem as if his staying here was bailing her out of a terrible jam, so what was he supposed to say?

Not until Trish, Hardy and little Laura had vanished did he recall that Hardy didn't have any family to speak of, none that he was in touch with anyway. With an able assist from Tyler, the whole lot of them had plotted against him again.

Okay, he thought, Tyler might be gone, Trish and her family had abandoned him, but there was still Dylan. Michael comforted himself with that. This time at least he wouldn't be out in the middle of nowhere without a familiar face in sight. And they'd left him with a working phone. He picked it up, listened suspiciously just in case they'd had the darn thing disconnected, then breathed a sigh of relief at the sound of the dial tone. He punched in his older brother's number.

But Dylan—surprise, surprise—was nowhere to be found.

"Off on a case," his wife said cheerfully. "Stop by while you're here, though. Bobby and I would love to see you. And if you need any help at the ranch, give me a call. My medical skills may be pretty much limited to kids, but I can rally a few of the Adamses who actually know a thing or two about horses and cattle. They'll be happy to come over to help out.''

Wasn't that just gosh-darn neighborly, Michael thought sourly as he sat on the porch in the gathering dusk and stared out at the field of wildflowers that Trish gushed about all the time. Frankly, he didn't get the fascination. They didn't *do* anything. Maybe after a couple of glasses of wine, he'd be more appreciative.

He was on his way inside in search of a decent cabernet and livelier entertainment, when he heard the distant cry. It sounded like someone in pain and it was coming from the barn, which should have been occupied by nothing more than a few of those horses Trish was so blasted worried about. Not that he was an expert, but no horse he'd ever heard sounded quite so human.

Adrenaline pumping, Michael eased around the house and slid through the shadows toward the small, neat barn. He could hear what sounded like muffled crying and a frantic exchange of whispers.

Thankful for his brother-in-law's skill in constructing the barn, he slid the door open in one smooth, silent glide and hit the lights, exposing two small, towheaded boys huddled in a corner, one of them holding a gashed hand to his chest, his face streaked with tears. Michael stared at them with astonishment and the unsettling sense that the day's bad luck was just about to take a spin for the worse.

''We ain't done anything, mister,'' the older boy said, facing him defiantly. Wearing a ragged T-shirt, frayed jeans and filthy sneakers, he stood protectively in front of the smaller, injured boy. The littler one gave Michael a hesitant smile, which faded when confronted by Michael's unrelenting scowl.

Michael's gaze narrowed. "What are you doing here?"

"We just wanted someplace to sleep for the night," the little one said, moving up to stand side by side with his companion whose belligerent expression now matched Michael's. His fierce loyalty reminded Michael of the four Delacourt brothers, whose one-for-all-and-all-for-one attitudes had gotten them into and out of a lot of sticky situations when they'd been about the same ages as these two.

"Come over here closer to the light and let me see your hand," he said to the smaller child, preferring to deal with the immediacy of an injury to the rest of the situation.

"It ain't nothing," the bigger boy said, holding him back.

"If it's bleeding, it's something," Michael replied. "Do you want it getting infected so bad, the doctors will have to cut off his arm?"

He figured the image of such an exaggeratedly gory fate would cut straight through their reluctance, but he'd figured wrong.

"We can fix it ourselves," the boy insisted stubbornly. "We found the first aid kit. I've already dumped lots and lots of peroxide over it."

"It hurt real bad, too," the little one said.

The comment earned him a frown, rather than praise for his bravery. "If he'd just hold still, I'd have it bandaged by now," the older boy grumbled.

"You two used to taking care of yourselves?" Michael asked, getting the uneasy sense that they'd frequently been through this routine of standing solidly together in defiance of adult authority.

The smaller boy nodded, even as the older one said a very firm, ''No.''

Michael bit back a smile at the contradictory responses. ''Which is it?''

''Look, mister, if you don't want us here, we'll go,'' the taller boy said, edging toward the door while keeping a safe distance between himself and Michael.

''What's your name?''

''I ain't supposed to tell that to strangers.''

''Well, seeing how you're on my property,'' he began, stretching the truth ever-so-slightly in the interest of saving time on unnecessary explanations about his own presence here. ''I think I have a right to know who you are.''

The boys exchanged a look before the older one finally gave a subtle nod.

''I'm Josh,'' the little one said. ''He's Jamie.''

''You two brothers?'' Michael asked.

''Uh-huh.''

''Do you have a last name, Josh and Jamie?''

''Of course, we do,'' Jamie said impatiently. ''But we ain't telling.''

Michael let that pass for the moment. ''Live around here?''

Again, he got two contradictory answers. He sighed. ''Which is it?''

''We're visiting,'' the little one said, as Jamie nodded. ''Yeah, that's it. We're visiting.''

Michael was an expert in sizing up people, reading their expressions. He wasn't buying that line of bull for a second. These two were runaways. There wasn't a doubt in his mind about that. Hadn't they just said they'd been looking for a place to spend the night? He decided to see how far they were willing to carry the fib.

"Won't the folks you're visiting be worried about you?" he asked. "Maybe we should call them."

"We're not sure of the number," Jamie said hurriedly, his expression worried.

"Tell me the name, then. I'll look it up."

"We can't," Jamie said. "They'll be real mad, when they find out we're gone. We weren't supposed to leave their place. They told us and told us not to go exploring, didn't they, Josh?"

"Uh-huh." Josh peered at Michael hopefully. "You don't want us to get in trouble, do you?"

Michael faced them with a stern, forbidding expression that worked nicely on the employees at Delacourt Oil. "No, what I want is the truth."

"That is the truth," Jamie vowed, sketching a cross over his heart and clearly not one bit intimidated.

"Honest," Josh said.

Michael feared he hadn't heard an honest, truthful word since these two had first opened their mouths. But if they wouldn't give him a straight answer, what was he supposed to do about it? He couldn't very well leave them in the barn. He couldn't send them packing, as desperately as he wanted to. They were just boys, no more than thirteen and nine, most likely. Somebody, somewhere, had to be worried sick about them. Maybe he could loosen their tongues with a bribe of food.

"You hungry?" he asked.

Josh's eyes lit up. His head bobbed up and down eagerly.

"I suppose we could eat," Jamie said, clearly trying hard not to show too much enthusiasm.

"Come on inside, then. Once you've eaten, we'll figure out where to go from there."

In Trish's state-of-the-art, spotless kitchen, they turned around in circles, wide-eyed with amazement.

"This is so cool," Jamie pronounced, his sullen defiance slipping away. "Like in a magazine or something."

"There's even a cookie jar," Josh announced excitedly. "A really big one. You suppose there are any cookies?"

"We'll check it out after you've eaten a sandwich," Michael said. He poured them both huge glasses of milk and made them thick ham and cheese sandwiches, which they fell on eagerly, either in anticipation of home-baked cookies or because they were half-starved.

Watching the boys while they devoured the food, Michael realized he needed advice and he needed it now. He needed an expert, somebody who understood kids, somebody who knew the law. Even as that realization struck him, he had a sudden inspiration. He knew the perfect person to get them all out of this jam. He walked into the living room, grabbed his portable phone and punched in a once-familiar number.

Grace Foster answered on the first ring, just as she always did. Grace was brisk and efficient. Best of all, she didn't play games. If she was home, why act as

if she had better things to do than talk? He'd liked
that about her once. Heck, he'd liked a whole lot
more than that about her, but that was another time,
another place, eons ago.

Now about all he could say was that he respected
her as a lawyer, even if she did make his life a living
hell from time to time.

"What do you want?" she asked the instant she
recognized his voice.

"Nice to speak to you, too," he countered.

"Michael, you never call unless there's a problem.
Since we don't have any court dates coming up, just
spit it out. It's Friday night. I'm busy."

"Whatever it is can wait," he retorted, troubled
more than he liked by the image of Grace being in
the midst of a hot date, one that might last all weekend long. He preferred to think that she led a nice,
quiet, solitary—*maidenly*—existence.

Although he'd intended only to ask for advice, instead he said, "I need you to get on a plane and get
over to Los Piños tonight."

He said it with absolute confidence that she
wouldn't refuse, not in the long run. She might grumble a little, but once she understood the stakes, she
wouldn't turn him down. He wondered just how little
he could get away with revealing. Maybe just the lure
of sparring with him would be enough. His ego certainly wanted to believe that.

"Excuse me? Why would I want to do that?" she
asked. "It's not like your every wish has been my
command, not for a long time now."

She employed that huffy little tone that always
turned him on although she intended the exact op-

posite. He could envision her sitting up a little straighter, squaring her shoulders. She had no idea that her efforts to look rigid and unyielding only thrust out her breasts and made her more desirable than ever. He bit back a desire to chuckle at the mental image. Grace was a real piece of work, all right. She might be pint-sized and fragile-looking, but she had the soul and spirit of a warrior. It was a trait he suspected was going to come in handy.

"You'll come because you know I wouldn't ask unless it was important," he told her patiently. Then he dangled an impossible-to-resist temptation. "And you can hold it over my head for the rest of our lives, okay?"

"Now that is an intriguing idea," she said with considerably more enthusiasm. "Care to fill me in?"

What a breeze, he thought triumphantly. Even easier than he'd anticipated. He hadn't even had to pull out the big guns and tell her about the kids.

"I'll fill you in when you get here. Can you be at the airport in an hour? I'll have the Delacourt jet fueled up and ready. The pilot can see to it that you find me once you land over here."

"Michael, really, there has to be someone else you could call, someone closer."

"There isn't," he assured her.

"But I have plans. I've had them for ages. I hate to cancel."

Damn, she was still trying to wriggle off the hook. "No," he said firmly. "It has to be you. This is right up your alley." He sighed heavily, then added as if it were costing him a great deal to say, "I need you, Grace."

"Hah! As if I believe that for a minute. You're overselling, Michael."

"Trust me. You're the only one for this job."

This time she was the one who sighed heavily. "Okay, okay. When you start laying it on this thick, my curiosity kicks in. But I have to finish up what I'm doing here. Make it ninety minutes," she said. "And, Michael, this is going to cost you. Big time."

"I never doubted it for a second," he said.

Only after he'd hung up did he stop to wonder why he'd instinctively turned to Grace, rather than his sister-in-law or one of the Adamses right here in town. He told himself it was because this situation all but cried out for a woman to deal with the two runaways, but he hadn't gotten where he was in life by deluding himself. His sister-in-law was not only obviously female, but a doctor, as well.

No, he had called Grace Foster, because as much of a pain in the butt as she was to him personally, she was the smartest lawyer he knew. If these boys were in some kind of trouble, he couldn't think of a better ally than Grace.

But it was even more than that, he admitted candidly. A part of him liked wrangling with Ms. Grace Foster more than just about anything except watching a new million-dollar gusher spewing crude into the Texas sky.

## Chapter Two

Grace could hardly wait to hear what had caused Michael Delacourt to condescend to beg her for help. As annoyed as she was at being imperiously summoned across the state on a Friday night, her curiosity had gotten the better of her.

And contrary to what she had deliberately led him to believe, he had not caught her in the middle of a pressing engagement. A long, boring weekend had stretched out ahead of her, so Michael's call had been a welcome diversion, a chance to break out of the rut she'd fallen into in recent months. She slaved like crazy in court all week long, then did more of the same on weekends so she wouldn't notice how truly barren her social life had become.

But even better than a break in routine, the promised chance to hold this over the man's arrogant, egotistical head for the rest of their lives had been an irresistible lure. Given the number of court cases on which they found themselves on opposing sides, it was an edge she couldn't ignore.

There was more to it, of course. There had been a time in the distant past when she had almost allowed herself to think about a future with Michael. But then she'd realized she would always play second fiddle to the family business. It was a role she flatly refused to accept.

Grace had already spent an entire childhood trying to figure out why she hadn't been smart enough or pretty enough for her father to love her. Norman Foster had left her and her mom when Grace was barely five. The unexplained departure of her adored father had all but destroyed her self-esteem. It had taken years to restore it, to accept that his going had had nothing at all to do with her. She wasn't going to waste the rest of her life wondering why she didn't have another man's full attention.

She had broken off with Michael the same day she'd graduated from law school. She'd had clues from the beginning of their relationship that work came first with him, but his failure to appear at the important graduation ceremony had made it all too evident where she fit into his priorities. Even his profuse apologies and a barrage of expensive gifts—all of which she'd returned—hadn't convinced her he would ever be able to change.

After pursuing her with flattering determination for a few weeks, he had accepted that the breakup was final. When he'd actually stopped calling, she'd suffered a few serious twinges of regret, but on balance she knew she'd done what she had to. She knew better than to think a man would change.

That didn't mean that she couldn't thoroughly enjoy the occasional sparring match with Michael. He was, after all, exceptionally smart, exceptionally sexy and, when he allowed himself to forget about work, highly entertaining. It gave her a great deal of pleasure, however, to remind him from time to time that he wasn't God's gift to women. She figured she had at least a little credibility since she was one of the few who'd ever walked away from him.

Over the years she had observed his pattern from a nice, safe distance. Most of the women he dated were eventually abandoned by him through benign neglect, never in an explosion of passionate fireworks. She suspected that most of those relationships contained less passion than some of the occasional conversations she and Michael had over legal matters. In the deep, dark middle of the night, she took a certain comfort in that.

Tonight as she settled into the fancy Delacourt corporate jet, she glanced around at the posh interior and smiled. Of course Michael expected her to be impressed by the bottle of chilled champagne, the little plate of hot hors d'oeuvres. No doubt he still thought of her as the small-town girl who'd been wide-eyed the first time he'd taken her on a trip in this very same plane.

They had gone from Austin, where she'd been in school, to Houston for a visit to the family mansion. Michael had wanted to introduce her to his family, especially his charismatic, much-idolized father. She had been stunned, if not impressed, by the evidence of their wealth. Even with Michael at her side, she had wondered if she would ever truly fit in there.

These days it took a lot more than champagne and canapés to impress her. Apparently Michael had forgotten that in recent years she'd worked for a lot of people every bit as rich as the Delacourts. In fact, she'd prided herself on taking quite a bit of money away from them.

Oh, yes, she thought with anticipation, this little trip to Los-wherever-Texas held a lot of promise. For Michael to be anywhere other than in his office or at some gala where he could network was so rare that the explanation was bound to be a doozy. She could hardly wait to hear it.

The flight didn't take long. When they landed, a car was waiting for her at the airport and the pilot gave her very thorough written and verbal directions, then regarded her anxiously.

"Are you sure you wouldn't like me to drive you, Ms. Foster? I don't mind, and Mr. Delacourt suggested that would be best."

Grace understood the insulting implications of that. She drew herself up to her full five-foot-two-inch height.

"Thanks, Paul, but I am perfectly capable of driving a few miles," she said coolly. Beyond his low regard for her driving skills, she knew what Michael was up to. He wanted her wherever he was at his beck and call, with no car available for a speedy exit. "Thank you, though. You can let Mr. Delacourt know that I am on my way."

The pilot, who'd been around during the days of their stormy relationship, grinned at her display of defiance. "Whatever you say, Ms. Foster. Nice seeing you again."

"You, too, Paul."

Satisfied that she had won that round, Grace got behind the wheel of the rental car, studied the directions one last time and tried not to panic. The truth was, she had a very unfortunate sense of direction. To top it off, the sky was pitch-black, the moon little more than a distant, shimmering sliver of silver. And it wasn't as if there were a lot of street signs out here in the middle of nowhere.

"I can do this," she told herself staunchly.

Twenty minutes later she was forced to concede that she was hopelessly lost. She drove around for another ten minutes trying to extricate herself from the tangle of rural roads that apparently led nowhere close to where she wanted to go. By the time she finally abandoned her pride, she was highly irritated. With great reluctance, she called Michael at the number the pilot had discreetly written at the bottom of the page.

"The plane landed forty-five minutes ago. Where the devil are you?" Michael demanded.

"If I knew that, I wouldn't be calling."

He moaned. "Don't tell me you've gotten yourself lost."

"It wasn't me," she protested. "It was these stupid directions. Whoever heard of telling somebody to turn at a blasted pine forest? I saw a pine tree, I turned. Now I seem to be staring at a pasture. There are cattle in the pasture, and I am not amused."

He chuckled.

"It's not funny. Laugh again and I'll be back at the airport and out of here."

"Not likely," he muttered.

"Michael," she said, her tone a warning.

"Sorry. It's just that this is one of your many charms," he said. "For a woman who has a law degree and a thriving practice in a major metropolitan area, you are absolutely pitiful when it comes to getting from one place to the next. I am amazed you ever make it to court on time."

"Will you just tell me how to get from here to there?" she snapped. She was not about to tell him that only years of practice and sticking to the same, precise route assured her of getting to the courthouse. Unanticipated detours gave her hives.

"Sweetheart, you're in a ranching area," he said, pointing out the obvious with what sounded like a little too much glee. "There are a lot of cows. Can't you just back up, turn around and get right back on the highway where you made the wrong turn?"

"You stay on the phone," she instructed. "I'll be back to you for further instructions when I am facing the highway."

It took another frustrating twenty minutes to backtrack and finally make her way to the turnoff Michael assured her would lead to where he was.

When she found him waiting for her on the front porch of a spectacular house with two boys sound asleep in the rocking chairs flanking him, her annoyance promptly gave way to amazement. This was obviously going to be a whole lot more fascinating than the weekend she'd anticipated spending with her case files and her law books.

\* \* \*

"Whose house is this and why are you here?" Grace asked as she and Michael settled in the living room with the cup of tea she'd insisted she preferred over wine. She wanted all her wits about her for this conversation.

"My brother-in-law built it for Trish," Michael explained. "And I'm here because I've got a whole family of conspirators."

"Another forced vacation?" She'd heard all about the last one. The tale had circled the Houston grapevine before landing in the society column of the daily paper. Imagining Michael's indignation, she had laughed out loud at the story, but she was wise enough to stifle a similar urge now.

"You don't have to look so amused," he said, his own expression thoroughly disgruntled.

"I guess even the high-and-mighty Michael Delacourt has someone he has to answer to on occasion."

"If you're going to start taking potshots, I'm going to regret calling you."

"It's all part of the package," she informed him. "But let's get down to business."

She gestured toward the stairs. The boys had been awakened and sent off to bed in a guest room. Since they'd barely been alert enough to acknowledge her existence, she imagined they were sleeping soundly again by now.

"Who are they?" she asked.

Michael appeared not to have heard her. They were alone in a cozy room that had been designed for the comfort of big men. He was sprawled in an oversized chair, looking frazzled. Even here he was dressed in slacks and a dress shirt with the sleeves rolled up and the collar open. No jeans and T-shirts for this man. No wonder he made the society pages so often. He always looked like a million bucks.

Grace liked her power suits as well as the next person, but on the weekends, she settled into shorts or comfortable, well-worn jeans, faded, shapeless T-shirts, and sandals. She'd deliberately worn her weekend wardrobe to demonstrate how unimpressed she'd been by this out-of-the-blue invitation.

Now, with her shoes kicked off, she was curled up in a matching chair opposite Michael regretting the fact that she'd left all those power suits at home. She could feel the tensions of the week easing away, right along with her defenses.

This was just a little too cozy. She'd barely resisted the urge to flip on every light in the room, so it was bathed only in the glow of a single lamp in the corner. The atmosphere was disturbingly romantic and Michael was enchantingly rumpled for a man who usually looked like he'd just stepped out of an ad for Armani suits. She had to force herself to concentrate on the topic at hand.

"Michael, who are they?" she asked again, when she realized his attention was focused intently on her. He looked as if he were trying to memorize every little detail about her. Under other circumstances it might have been flattering. Under these circumstances, it rattled her in a way she didn't want to be rattled.

His gaze finally snapped up. "Jamie and Josh,"

he replied. "Beyond that, your guess is as good as mine. They refused to disclose a last name."

"Smart kids. It'll slow you down tracing where they belong. Any idea where that might be?"

"Not a one. I found them in the barn."

She was relieved to be able to finally slip into lawyer mode. "Like a couple of stray cats?" she asked. "Or burgling the place?"

"Looking for a place to sleep, they said."

"Did you believe them?"

"I believe they weren't there to steal anything. I also believe they're in some sort of trouble. They wouldn't give me a clue about where they came from, wouldn't let me call anyone to let them know they were okay. They claimed to be visiting in the area, but they wouldn't give me a name."

"Runaways," Grace deduced, her heart aching. She'd seen the sorry state of their clothes. More than that, she'd detected the worry in their eyes that not even being half-asleep could disguise. They had to be exhausted if they were risking sleep. Otherwise they'd probably be at the top of the stairs eavesdropping or slipping out an upstairs window as she and Michael discussed their fate.

"Looks that way to me," Michael agreed.

"Have you checked the local paper, turned on TV to see if they've been reported missing?"

"No, I just called you."

"Why?" she asked, bewildered by him turning to her. She would have expected him to go straight to his family. With the Delacourt resources, including a private eye for a brother, wouldn't that have made more sense? Even if he was ticked at most of them at the moment, they were the closest, most obvious people to call.

"What about Dylan?" she asked. "Isn't he living over here now?"

"He's away."

"And Trish? Maybe she knew about the boys hiding out in the barn but didn't say anything."

"I can't imagine Trish going off and leaving two runaways behind. She'd have brought them in and mothered them to death," he said wryly.

"Maybe you should call her and ask."

He looked vaguely uncomfortable. "Not a good idea."

"Why not?"

A scowl settled on his face again. "Because, if you must know, I have no idea where she is. She deliberately kept me in the dark about her destination. Made up a bunch of hogwash that turned out not to be true."

"So that makes me what? Third choice after Dylan and Trish?"

"Nope, first," he insisted. "Like I told you on the phone, this is right up your alley. You know about all this family law stuff. You're compassionate. You're a woman."

"And your sister-in-law, Dylan's wife, is *what?*" she asked wryly. Because the Delacourts were big news in Houston, she'd been able to keep up. She knew all about their marriages.

Michael shrugged off the question, as if it wasn't worthy of a response.

"Unreachable by phone?" she suggested. "Out in the hinterlands delivering a baby, perhaps?"

"I don't know. I didn't try. Look, Grace, I know this is an imposition, but you're the best. Face it, I'm out of my element. When that happens, I know enough to call in an expert."

If she'd been on her feet, she'd probably have fainted at the admission. "That has to be a first," she commented.

"What?"

"You admitting you're at a loss."

He regarded her evenly. "I'm not blind to my faults, Grace."

"Just not interested in correcting them?" she surmised.

His gaze narrowed. "Do you really want to take that particular walk down memory lane?"

Her cheeks burned. She swallowed hard and shook her head, reminding herself that his calling her wasn't personal. He hadn't dragged her over here because he'd been pining away for her for the past few years. It was about those two scared boys upstairs. Nothing else. Period. She had to keep that in mind. It would be way too easy to get caught up in all of this, to imagine that they were partners, a team…a family.

No sooner had that thought slammed into her head, than she jerked herself sternly back to reality. They were nothing to each other. *Nothing.* Old friends, at best. And this weekend was nothing more than a tiny, last-gasp blip on their flat-lined relationship. It was not evidence that there was life in it.

"No, of course not," she said briskly.

"I thought not." He studied her intently. "So, what do I do with them?"

He sounded genuinely perplexed, as if the decision-making king of the business world had finally butted up against a problem he couldn't solve with a snap of his fingers or a flurry of memos. Grace found the uncertainty more appealing than she cared to admit. For Michael Delacourt to show his vulnerability, especially to her, was something worth noting.

"What options have you considered?" she asked, curious to know exactly where he was coming from. "And speaking of experts, why didn't you just call the police and let them deal with the situation?"

To her relief, he looked genuinely appalled by the suggestion.

"They're a couple of scared kids. How could I call the police? They haven't done anything wrong."

"They've run away for starters, and you don't know that they haven't done more," she pointed out realistically. "They could have been roaming around for weeks breaking into places, stealing food, jewelry and who knows what else."

"If they were stealing food, they weren't much good at it. They were starved," he said, ignoring the rest.

"Think back, Michael. All boys that age are starved at least a half-dozen times a day," she reminded him.

"Yeah, I suppose you're right."

She was still mystified by what he expected. "Look, Michael, what exactly do you want me to do?"

"Talk to them. Handle it. Figure out what's going on. Get them back home." He raked his hand through his thick, dark brown hair in a gesture of frustration that pretty much destroyed the usual neat style. "I don't know."

She found that appealing, too. Because her reaction irritated her, she snapped, "Just get them off your plate and onto mine, I suppose."

His expression brightened. "Exactly."

"Sorry, pal," she said, getting to her feet. She needed to get out of here before she succumbed to Michael's charm and the very real distress of those two boys. This was heartache she didn't need. There were plenty of other people around who could step in here and solve this, professionals with nothing at stake except doing their jobs.

"I think handling a couple of kids ought to be a piece of cake for a man who controls a multinational corporation," she said. "You'll be good for each other. Consider it your good deed for the century. Just think, you'll have it out of the way right at the start."

With the pointed barb delivered, she skirted past him and aimed for the door. Conveniently, her overnight bag was still there. She'd barely made a grab for it, though, when he stepped into her path. Even though Michael went through life with an economy of movements, he had always been able to move as swiftly as a panther when he chose to. Apparently right now he was highly motivated.

"You can't leave," he protested.

"Oh, but I can."

"Grace, don't do this to me. You're a lawyer. You know how to cut through red tape, get things done."

She regarded him with amusement. "And you

don't? Please. Compared to convincing a foreign government to let you steal mineral rights, this is just a little inconvenience. Deal with it.''

"Do you want me to beg?"

She grinned at the prospect, then regarded him curiously. "An interesting possibility. Are you any good at it?"

"Let me give it a shot."

He reached for her hand, pressed a kiss against her knuckles that sent shockwaves cavorting right through her. It wasn't exactly begging, but she had to admit it was an excellent start. Something inside her was melting right along with her resolve.

"Please, Grace. Stick around through the weekend at least. Help me get a straight story out of those kids. Once we've figured out what to do, you can race straight back to Houston and I won't bother you again for another half-dozen years or so."

She withdrew her hand, because she didn't like the sensations his touch was kicking off. "Nice try, but I'm not convinced yet that you really need me. Any old lawyer would do. Doesn't Delacourt Oil have a slew of them on retainer?"

He frowned at that. "None like you."

She regarded him with surprise. "I almost believe you mean that."

"Believe me, Grace, I have never meant anything more, never needed you more," he said with convincing solemnity. "Never."

There was a time when those words would have made her pulse ricochet wildly. Unfortunately, they still had a disconcerting effect. Ignoring it, she shook her head and took another step back, a step toward putting a safe emotional distance between them.

"Maybe this will be good for you, Michael. Put you in touch with real human beings for a change."

He appeared genuinely offended by the implication. "I deal with real human beings all the time."

"You just don't find them nearly as interesting as the bottom line, is that it?"

"You're not being fair."

"Probably not," she agreed. "But we both know life isn't always fair."

His gaze locked on hers. "But you are, Grace. Fairness is what you're all about. You fight for the underdog. Nobody knows that better than I do. I've seen you take some of my friends to the cleaners to make sure their ex-wives get what they deserve. Hell, you've taken me apart on the witness stand to pry out some ugly truths about friends of mine. We both know how tough you are when it matters. You handled that situation for Jeb's wife when you thought the company was misjudging her. If it hadn't been straightened out to your satisfaction, you would have fought like a tiger for her."

"You lucked out. Brianna was in love with Jeb and he was smart enough to go to bat for her in the end. Otherwise we would have sued your pants off and won."

He grinned. "That's what I mean. You don't care *who* you go up against, if you think the cause is just."

"There's a difference this time," she said.

"What's different?"

"You and I would be on the same side. I think I

like it better when we're battling on opposite sides,'' she admitted candidly.

"Safer that way?" he inquired, an all-too-knowing glint in his eyes.

She was surprised that he could read her so well. "Smarter," she corrected.

He regarded her with amusement. "You don't still have a thing for me, do you, Grace? Being here with me isn't dredging up old memories, is it?"

She bristled at the suggestion. "Of course not."

"Then it shouldn't be a problem, right?" he said, clearly laying down a challenge. "We'll leave the past off-limits, stick strictly to the situation at hand."

It rankled that he thought it would be so easy to avoid rekindling their old passion. But if he could spend this weekend with her and keep it impersonal, then she certainly could...or she would die trying.

"Fine," she said, picking up her bag again, this time turning toward the stairs. "Okay, where's my room? Since I'm staying, I'm obviously too beat to think straight. We'll tackle this in the morning."

And in the morning, maybe she'd be able to figure out why Michael Delacourt was the only male on earth who could still twist her right around his finger without even trying.

## Chapter Three

Michael had never been so relieved to see anyone in his life as he had been to see Grace pull into the driveway the night before. The fact that his heart had done a little hop, skip and jump had been gratitude, nothing more, he assured himself. The woman was far too prickly for him to consider another run at anything more, especially when there were plenty of willing women who'd be grateful for his attention and who wouldn't grumble if he had to cancel a date every now and again.

Not that he didn't understand why Grace had been furious when he'd missed her law school graduation years ago. He'd known exactly how important that day was to her. She had struggled and sacrificed to go to college, worked herself to a frazzle to succeed.

She had earned that moment of triumph, and he should have been there to witness it.

Even understanding all that, he'd gotten caught up in a tough negotiation and hadn't even glanced at a clock until it was too late to make the ceremony. He'd apologized in every way he could think of, but she'd been unforgiving. Still was, as far as he could tell.

At the time, he'd told himself it was for the best. After all, how could a man in his position be expected to work nine to five? If he followed the workaholic example set by his father, his career was destined to be time-consuming. If Grace was going to be unreasonably demanding, it would never work out. Better to find that out before they were married.

He winced when he thought of how he'd tried to deftly shift all of the blame to her, tried to make her feel guilty for his neglect, as if it were her expectations that were at fault, not his insensitivity. No wonder she'd taken every opportunity since to make him squirm in court. He was amazed that she'd shown up here at all, much less stayed. But, then, Grace had too much grit, too much honor, to let her distaste for him stand in the way of helping someone truly in need.

One glance at those two boys and Michael had seen her heart begin to melt. Despite her tough exterior, she was a soft touch. Always had been. Even when she'd been struggling to pay tuition, refusing to accept so much as a dime from him, she'd never been able to turn away a lost kitten or a stray dog. She'd craved family the way some people needed sex. He'd counted on that to work in his favor when he'd called her.

And speaking of sex, being in such close proximity to her was going to be sheer torture. Just because he'd recognized that they weren't suited for marriage didn't mean that recognition shut off his hormones. The minute she'd stepped out of that rental car, looking annoyed and disheveled, he'd promptly envisioned her in bed with him, and in this scenario he was doing some very clever and inventive things to put a smile back on her face. He doubted she would have been pleased to know the direction of his thoughts.

He was none too pleased about them himself, since he'd been in an uncomfortable state of arousal ever since his first glimpse of her the night before. He figured an icy shower was going to be his only salvation and, if Grace was sticking around, he might as well get used to taking them. Uncontrollable lust or not, he had no intention of strolling down that particular dead-end road again. He had trouble enough on his hands with Jamie and Josh under his roof—or Trish's roof, to be more precise about it.

He considered hanging around upstairs for a while longer, giving her plenty of time to solve the problem of the runaway kids, but guilt had him showered and dressed and on his way downstairs just after dawn. To his surprise, he was the last one up.

When he wandered into the kitchen, he found Grace blithely flipping pancakes for two wide-eyed and eager boys, whose blond hair had been slicked back and whose faces had been scrubbed clean. Grace's influence, no doubt.

They were currently falling all over themselves to get the table set for her. Given the fact that she was barefoot and had chosen to dress in shorts and a T-shirt, he could understand their reaction. He was pretty darned anxious to do whatever he could to please her, too. Unfortunately, his ideas would have to wait for another time, another place…probably another lifetime.

"Grace says as soon as we eat, we're going to talk about what to do with us," Josh announced, sounding surprisingly upbeat about the prospect. Obviously he was crediting Grace with the good judgment not to do anything against his will.

"We're not going back," Jamie inserted direly, his gaze pointedly resting first on Michael, then on Grace. "So, if that's what you're thinking, you can forget it."

Obviously he was not as willing to assume Michael's good will or Grace's powers of persuasion as his little brother was.

"Back to where?" Michael asked, hoping to get a quick, uncensored response.

Grace shot a warning look at him. "That's enough for now. We'll talk about it after breakfast," she soothed, a hand resting gently on the boy's shoulder. "We'll all be able to think more clearly after we've eaten. How many pancakes, Jamie?"

"Four," he said, his distrust clearly not extending to the matter of food.

"I want five," Josh said.

"You can't eat five," Jamie countered. "You're littler than me."

"Can so."

"How about you both start with four and see if you want more?" Grace suggested, deftly averting a full-scale war between the two boys. She turned her attention to Michael for the first time since he'd entered the kitchen. "And you?"

"Just coffee. Lots and lots of coffee."

"The pancake offer only goes around once," she advised him. "I'll give you four, too. You look like you could use a decent breakfast for a change. You probably have the executive special back home."

"What's that?" Josh asked.

"Half a grapefruit and dry toast," Grace said with obvious distaste. "Keeps them lean and mean."

"Oh, yuck," both boys agreed in unison.

It was too close to the truth for Michael to contradict Grace's guesswork or the boys' disgust. "Whatever," he mumbled, pouring himself a cup of coffee and taking his first sip gratefully. It was strong, just the way he liked it.

When they were all seated at the round kitchen table, plates piled high with pancakes that had been drowned in maple syrup, Grace regarded Michael with interest. "In all the confusion last night, I forgot to ask. Where exactly are we? You said Los Piños on the phone. The pilot neglected to give me any details about our flight plan."

"And we all know your sense of direction is seriously flawed," Michael teased. "Los Piños is in west Texas. That's the opposite side of the state from Houston, in case you were wondering."

"How exactly did Trish manage to lure you over here before deserting you?"

"She didn't. Tyler came into my office and

nagged until he got me on the company jet under the pretense of bringing me over here for a big family reunion.''

''And you bought that, after what they did to you last time?'' she asked, looking incredulous.

''What happened last time?'' Josh asked, his face alight with curiosity, his overloaded fork hovering in midair.

''They took him off to a cabin in the woods and left him,'' Grace said with a certain amount of obvious delight. ''One whole week.''

''Cool,'' Jamie declared.

''No cell phone. No TV. No newspapers. No financial news,'' Grace added cheerily, as if she knew exactly what had driven him up a wall during those seven endless days. ''Did they stock the refrigerator, or were you expected to catch your dinner in the lake?''

Michael scowled at her but didn't bother to reply. He was not about to discuss his lack of expertise with a fishing rod or the fact that Trish had left him with a freezer filled with meals prepared and labeled, complete with microwave instructions.

''No TV?'' Josh asked with evident shock. ''What did you do?''

''Cursed my family for the most part,'' Michael said. He'd also read half the books on the shelves, even the classics that he'd avoided back in school. ''Could we drop the sorry saga of my sneaky relatives, please? Just thinking about it is giving me indigestion.''

''What amazes me is not their sneakiness, but your gullibility,'' Grace said, ignoring his plea to end the topic. "Once, maybe, but twice? That radar of yours must be slipping, Michael. You've obviously lost your edge. I hope none of your competitors get wind of that."

He frowned at her taunt. "My edge is just fine, thank you. I got you over here, didn't I?"

She laughed. "Touché."

"What does that mean?" Josh asked.

"It means he got the last laugh, at least for now," Grace told him. "Now eat. Your pancakes are getting cold."

Jamie regarded Michael worriedly. "If you're here on some kind of vacation, does that mean this place ain't yours?"

"No, it *isn't* mine," Michael said, in a probably wasted attempt to correct the boy's pitiful grammar. "It belongs to my sister."

"Oh," Jamie said flatly. He looked as disappointed as if Michael had revealed that there was no Santa Claus. Of course, these two probably hadn't believed in Santa for quite some time, if ever.

"Does that bother you for some reason?" Grace asked Jamie.

"It's just that it's real nice, the nicest place we've been in a while. Even the barn was real clean."

"Were you hoping to stick around?" Grace inquired casually.

"Maybe," Jamie admitted, clearly struggling to keep any hint of real hope out of his voice. "For a little bit. Just till we figure out what to do next. I gotta get a job if I'm gonna take care of me and Josh."

Michael was about to question what sort of a job

he expected to get at his age, but Grace gave him a subtle signal, as if she knew what he'd been about to say and wanted him to keep silent.

"Where's home for you guys?" she asked instead, sneaking in the very same question she'd wanted Michael to back away from earlier.

"Ain't got one," Jamie said, returning her gaze belligerently.

"Okay, then, where did you run away from?" When they didn't answer, she said, "You might as well tell us. Otherwise, we'll just have to call the police so they can check all the missing persons reports."

Josh regarded them worriedly. "If we say, can we stay here? I can do laundry and make my bed. We won't be any trouble. Honest."

It was already too late for that, Michael thought. He was harboring two runaways and a woman he had a desperate desire to kiss senseless. Talk about a weekend fraught with danger.

"No," he said a little too sharply. He saw the look of betrayal in their eyes and felt like a heel. Before he could stop himself, he moderated the sharp refusal. "Tell us the truth and then we'll talk about what happens next."

"You'll really listen to what we got to say?" Jamie asked skeptically.

"We'll listen," Grace promised.

"We gotta tell," Josh said, regarding his big brother stubbornly. "Maybe they'll let us stay."

"I say we don't," Jamie insisted. "They're grown-ups. They'll just make us go back. They'll say they gotta, because it's the law or something. You want to be separated again, like last time?''

He seemed unaware of just how revealing his question was. Michael was uncomfortably aware of an ache somewhere in the region of his heart. These two were getting to him, no doubt about it. As for Grace, they'd clearly already stolen her heart. She was regarding them sympathetically.

''You were in foster care, weren't you?'' she guessed. ''And not together?''

''Uh-huh,'' Josh said, shooting a defiant look at his brother. ''Nobody would take both of us last time or the time before that. They said we were too much trouble when we were together.''

''I'm old enough to look out for my own kid brother,'' Jamie said, regarding them both with his usual belligerence. ''We'll be okay. You don't have to do nothin'. Soon as we eat, we'll go.''

''Go where?'' Michael asked, feeling as if the kids had sucker punched him. He tried to imagine being separated from Dylan, Jeb and Tyler when they'd been the ages of these boys. He couldn't. They were bound together by a shared history, by family and by the kind of fierce love and loyalty that only siblings felt despite whatever rivalries existed.

He focused his attention on Jamie, since he was clearly the leader. Josh would trustingly go along with whatever his big brother wanted. ''How old are you?''

''Sixteen,'' Jamie said, drawing a shocked look from his brother.

''I'd guess thirteen, tops,'' Michael said, turning to gauge Josh's reaction, rather than Jamie's. The boy gave him a subtle but unmistakable nod. "How about you, Josh? Eight? Nine?"

"Eight," Josh admitted readily. He was apparently eager to provide any information that might persuade Michael and Grace to keep the two of them at the ranch. "Last week. That's when Jamie came for me, on my birthday. We've always been together on our birthdays, no matter what. We promised."

"And that's a very good promise to try to keep," Grace said. "Families should stick together whenever they can."

As she said it, she kept her gaze locked on Michael. He got the message. There were now evidently three against one in the room should he decide to fight for an immediate call to the proper authorities. Grace wasn't going to turn these two over to anybody who would separate them again, though how she hoped to avoid it was beyond him. There were probably a zillion rules about how to handle this, and he'd brought her here precisely because she knew them. Now she was showing every indication that she might just ignore all zillion of them. For the moment, however, it had to be her call. She was the expert.

"How long have you been in foster care?" she asked, apparently inferring from Michael's silence that he was willing to withhold judgment until all the facts were in.

"Since Josh was four," Jamie finally confessed. "We were together in the first place, but then they got mad at me, 'cause I wouldn't follow all their stupid rules, so I got sent away to another family. They kept Josh till he ran away to find me. When they dragged him back, he cried and cried, till he made himself sick. Then they said they couldn't cope with him either.''

Michael swallowed hard at the image of a little boy sobbing his heart out for his big brother. Instead of being treated with compassion, he'd been sent away. What kind of monsters did that to a child? He glanced at Grace and thought he detected tears in her eyes.

"How many places have you been since then?" she asked gently.

"Four," Jamie said without emotion. "Josh has been in three."

"Because you keep running away to be together?" Grace concluded.

"Uh-huh."

"What happened to your parents?"

"We don't got any," Jamie said flatly. His sharp gaze dared his brother to contradict him.

Even so, Josh couldn't hide his shock at the reply. "That's not true," he protested, fighting tears. "We got a mom. You know we do."

"For all the good it does. She's been in rehab or jail as far back as I can remember," Jamie said angrily. "What good is a mom like that?"

"I'm sure she loves you both very much, despite whatever problems she has," Grace said. "Sometimes things just get to be overwhelming and people make mistakes."

"Yeah, like turning her back on her own kids," Jamie said with resentment. "Some mistake."

Michael was inclined to agree with him, but he kept silent. This was Grace's show. She no doubt

knew what to say under very complicated circumstances like this. He didn't have a clue. He just knew
he wanted to crack some adult heads together. The
vehemence of his response surprised him. Grace was
the champion of the underdog, not him. He'd wanted
to distance himself from this situation, not get drawn
more deeply into it. But with every word Jamie and
Josh spoke, he could feel his defenses crumbling.

"Where are you from—I mean originally, back
when you lived with your mom?" Grace asked the
boys.

The question surprised him. He'd just assumed the
boys had to be from someplace nearby. How else
would they have wound up in Trish and Hardy's
barn? Realistically, though, how many foster homes
were there likely to be around Los Piños? How much
need for them would there be in a town this size,
anyway?

"We were born in San Antonio," Jamie said.
"But we moved around a lot, even before Mom
ditched us. I can't even remember all the places. She
liked big cities best because it was easier to get…"
He shrugged. "You know…stuff."

Michael was very much afraid he did know. He
held back a sigh.

"And your last foster home?" Grace asked. "Was
it near here?"

The boy shook his head. "Not really. When I got
Josh, I figured this time we'd better get far away so
they could never find us. I figured they'd just give
up after a couple of days. It's not as if anybody really
cares where we are. We've been hitching rides for a
while now. Like a week, maybe."

"Yeah," Josh said. "We must have gone about a thousand miles."

"It's only a couple of hundred, doofus," Jamie said.

"Well, it seems like a lot. We didn't get a lot of rides, so we had to walk and walk. Jamie wouldn't get in a car with just anybody. He said we could only get in pickups where we could ride in the back."

Michael listened, horrified. He saw the same sense of dismay on Grace's face. Clearly, they both knew all too well what might have happened to two small boys on the road alone. Obviously Jamie, at his age and with his street smarts, understood the dangers as well, but it was also clear that he thought those were preferable to another bad foster care experience or another separation.

"We told the truth," Jamie said, looking from Grace to Michael and back again. "You gonna let us stay?" He didn't sound especially hopeful. His expression suggested he was ready to run at the first hint that Michael and Grace might not agree to let them stick around.

"Why don't you boys go and check on the feed for the horses?" Michael suggested. "Grace and I need to talk things over and decide what's best." He scowled at Jamie. "And don't get any ideas about taking off while we do, okay? We'll work this out. I promise."

He meant that promise more than he'd ever meant anything in his life.

Unfortunately, he had a feeling that the solution to this particular problem wasn't going to come to them over a second cup of coffee. And judging from Grace's troubled expression, she knew it, too.

## Chapter Four

Grace wanted to cry. As the boys straggled deject-
edly out of the kitchen as if the weight of the world
were on their narrow shoulders, she couldn't bear to
meet Michael's gaze. She was afraid if she did, the
tears would come and she wouldn't be able to stop
them.

She identified with Josh and Jamie a little too
much. She could remember exactly what it felt like
to have no one around she could count on. After her
father's departure, her mother had sunk more and
more deeply into a depression from which she never
recovered. Grace had been eighteen when her mother
died, a sad, lost woman.

Because for so many years Grace had been as
much caregiver as child, she had felt the loss even
more deeply, felt even more abandoned and alone.

She blinked back tears at the memory of that time. She had been so frightened and so determined not to show it.

That was when she had met Michael and, for a time, she had felt connected. She had leaned on him, drawing strength from the attention he had showered on her, envisioning herself a part of his large family even though at that time she'd never met them.

But, in the end, he hadn't been able to give her what she desperately needed—a storybook family in which she would come first with him, just as he did with her. Graduation day had been a brutal awakening for her. She had realized then that the only person she could truly count on was herself. She'd clung to her independence ever since, not wanting to risk more disillusionment with another man.

But while her lifestyle suited her now, she didn't want that for Jamie and Josh, who were already far too used to fending for themselves. She wanted them to be surrounded by people who cared, people they knew would be there for them always.

"Grace?"

Michael's concerned voice drew her back to the present. "What?" she said without glancing up.

"You okay?"

"Of course," she said, forcing a brisk, confident note into her voice. It was her courtroom tone, the one she drew on so no judge or jury would ever sense a hint of vulnerability. Even so, she wasn't quite ready to look him in the eye.

"This is a hell of a mess, isn't it?" he said.

"Now there's an understatement, if ever I heard one."

"What are we going to do?"

Her gaze came up at that. *"We?"* she echoed, not bothering to hide her surprise. "I thought you intended to dump this into my lap."

"Look, if you don't want my help, that's fine by me. Believe me, nothing would please me more that to turn this over to you and get on with my nice, peaceful vacation."

She regarded him skeptically. " 'Peaceful' and 'vacation' are not two words I normally associate with you," she said. "You're here under duress, remember?"

"The prospect has become considerably more appealing overnight."

"How unfortunate, since we have a crisis on our hands," she declared, emphatically echoing him.

"I knew it was a mistake the minute I said that," he muttered.

He didn't sound half as disgruntled as she was sure he meant to. In fact, he sounded like a man who'd unwillingly been deeply touched by what those boys had already been through in their young lives. For the first time ever, she thought maybe she knew Michael Delacourt better than he knew himself. She had always known that he possessed a heart. He just wasn't in touch with it very often. He wouldn't allow himself to be, because he wanted nothing to compete with the time he devoted to Delacourt Oil.

Those boys had reached him in a way she suspected he rarely allowed to happen. She wasn't about to let him back away from the experience. Just as he was about to rise from his seat—probably intent on beating a hasty retreat—she put her hand on his.

"Oh, no, you don't. You're not getting out of this that easily."

He sank back down with a sigh of resignation, then reached for a piece of paper. "Okay, what's the game plan?" he asked.

He sounded as if he were strategizing a corporate takeover and wanted every detail nailed down in advance. He almost seemed eager to get started. Or maybe, she thought more realistically, he was simply anxious to get finished.

Despite Michael's sense of urgency, Grace considered their options thoughtfully. "I'm going to make a few discreet inquiries," she began slowly.

He regarded her worriedly, as if he already sensed that he wasn't going to like the role she had in mind for him. "What about me?"

She regarded him with a certain amount of delight. "You're going to go out there and see how much more information you can pry out of Josh and Jamie."

"Such as?"

"A last name would be helpful. So would their mother's name."

"Grace, those two fell in love with you at first sight. They were all but falling all over themselves earlier to please you. If they wouldn't talk to you, how do you expect me to get them to open up? They don't trust me. The only reason they didn't sneak away from here last night was because they were too exhausted to try."

"It's not too late to change that. You can become their new best buddy." She looked him over carefully. He was in another pair of slacks with creases so sharp they could have cut butter and a shirt that probably cost more than everything in her suitcase. "One little suggestion, though, before you go outside."

"I could use more than one suggestion, sweetheart. I need a damned manual."

"You were a boy once, Michael. You had brothers. Surely you recall what that was like."

"Of course, but Jamie and Josh are nothing like we were."

"For good reasons."

"I know that. What I don't know is how to get through to them, especially Jamie. He's got solid concrete walls built around himself."

"Are you surprised?"

"Of course not, but—"

"Michael, give it up. You're a bright man. You can do this. For starters, how about changing into a pair of jeans and some boots? Dressed like that, you'd intimidate a CEO. That outfit might be fine for an afternoon at the country club, but out here you are seriously overdressed."

To her surprise he chuckled.

"What's so funny?"

"I was wondering how long it was going to take before you tried to get me out of my clothes." He winked at her on his way out of the room. "Turned out to take a whole lot less time than I'd imagined."

Michael's taunting good humor was short-lived. He exited the house in the jeans and scuffed boots he normally wore to the oil fields feeling about as confident as a man facing a firing squad.

He stood silently for a moment, drawing in a deep breath of the scented morning air. He had a feeling it was the first time in years he'd actually been aware of the air he was breathing. The last time had probably been at the beach house where he'd always enjoyed sitting on the porch with a cup of coffee and the scent of salty sea breezes surrounding him.

"Whatcha doing?" Josh asked, slipping up beside him and regarding him curiously.

"Trying to decide what that scent in the air is," he admitted. "Take a deep breath and see if you can tell."

Josh gave an exaggerated sniff. "Must be those roses over there," he said, indicating a garden Michael hadn't noticed before. "They smell real sweet, just like that."

Michael laughed.

Josh stared at him. "What's so funny?"

"Some would say it's about time I stopped to smell the roses," Michael told him.

"What's that mean?"

"It means I'm usually too busy to pay attention to what's going on around me."

The boy nodded. "One of my foster dads was like that. He was never home. Sometimes he stayed out all night. When he did, my foster mom would cry."

Michael doubted Josh had any idea what the man had probably been up to on those nights away from home. Obviously, though, seeing his foster mom cry had troubled him. He gave the boy's shoulder a sympathetic squeeze. "That must have been tough on you."

"Yeah, well, when you're a foster kid, you get used to stuff," he said with a shrug.

Michael resolved then and there that there would be no more *stuff* for Josh and Jamie to learn to take in stride. He would do whatever it took to see that they landed in a good home this time, maybe even try to make them eligible for adoption if their mother wasn't ever going to get her life straightened out. The courts were looking more favorably on making that happen these days, rather than leaving children in limbo forever. Whatever he and Grace decided to do, though, they had to move quickly, before logic got all tangled up with emotion.

He glanced down and saw that Josh was mimicking his wide stance, his hands locked behind his back just as Michael's were. He bit back a sudden desire to smile.

"Where's Jamie?" he asked Josh.

"In the barn. He's not touching anything," he assured Michael hurriedly. "Just looking."

"Looking is fine," Michael assured him. "Does he like horses?"

Josh's head bobbed up and down. "He loves horses more than anything. He really, really wants to learn to ride," he confided. "Even more than me. Do you think we could? Could you teach us?"

What was it with everyone trying to get him on a blasted horse? Michael wondered.

"We'll see," he hedged, then felt terrible when he saw the disappointment rising in Josh's eyes. Maybe he could get someone from White Pines over here to give the boys lessons. He couldn't do that, though, until he and Grace had made some progress in finding out their legal status. That had to be cleared up before everyone landed in a heap of trouble.

"I'll make you a deal," he said, hunkering down until he was at eye level with Josh. He'd pulled off multimillion dollar negotiations with less finesse than this conversation was likely to require.

"What kind of a deal?" Josh asked, regarding him with innate distrust.

"You tell me your last name so Grace and I can get your situation straightened out, and I'll get someone over here to give you riding lessons."

"I don't know," Josh replied, clearly torn. "Jamie would be real mad if he found out."

"Jamie wants to ride. Maybe he'd consider it a fair trade-off."

Obviously tempted, Josh brightened. "Let's go ask him," he said, tugging on Michael's hand.

Michael had a feeling Jamie's hide was tougher than Josh's. No matter how badly he wanted the riding lessons, Jamie might not be willing to tell Michael what he needed to know.

"No," Michael said, halting their forward motion. "This deal is between the two of us. I won't tell your brother you told me."

"But he'll know," Josh reasoned. "How else could you find out?"

"If he asks, I'll tell him I had my brother do some research. He's a private investigator."

"But that's a lie."

Michael winced at his shock. "I know, but once in a very long while, when it's to protect someone's feelings, a very small lie is okay."

Josh was still hesitant. "But I promised I wouldn't tell. Not ever."

"Some promises can be broken if it's for a really, really good reason," Michael reassured him. He couldn't help wondering if he wasn't teaching Josh to bend way too many of the values he'd been taught. Maybe these were lessons that should have waited until he was old enough to make the right distinctions about the circumstances. Too late now, though.

Josh regarded him worriedly. "You swear we'll get to ride the horses?"

"Cross my heart," Michael said, sketching a cross across his chest.

Josh beckoned him closer. Michael bent down. "Miller," he whispered. "That's our last name. Our mom is Naomi Miller."

"Josh!"

The shout of betrayal echoed across the corral. Neither of them had seen Jamie emerge from the barn. Whether he had heard all of the words from that distance or not, he clearly suspected that Josh was confiding something he shouldn't.

Before Michael could react, Jamie raced across the ground and tackled his brother, throwing him to the ground, then landing on top of him, fists flying.

For a moment, Josh gave as good as he got, but Jamie was bigger and stronger. When Michael figured the odds were way too uneven, he reached down and snagged Jamie by the back of his shirt. The boy came to his feet flailing at Michael. One punch caught him squarely in the jaw, jarring his teeth. He figured it was no more than he deserved for his role in this.

"Enough!" Grace commanded, appearing out of nowhere, her voice calm but unyielding.

Jamie stilled, but the anger in his eyes continued to cast sparks in Michael's direction.

"What is this all about?" she demanded, her gaze on Michael.

Jamie and Josh stared at him, clearly wary of what he might say.

"Just a little disagreement," he said mildly. "Nothing to get excited about."

"It is not a little disagreement when Josh has the beginnings of a black eye and cuts all over him and you're rubbing a swollen jaw." Her gaze landed on Jamie. "Well?"

"I'm not telling," he said sullenly. He stared pointedly at his brother. "I don't tell secrets."

Josh flushed, tears welling up in his eyes.

Michael sighed. The last thing he'd meant to do was cause a rift between the brothers. He knew it wouldn't last, but for now they were both hurting in ways well beyond whatever physical injuries they'd suffered.

"This is my fault," he confessed.

Grace stared at him in surprise. "It is? Why?"

"I asked Josh for some information. We made a deal. It was a fair deal, but I should never have put him in that position," he said candidly. He regarded both boys intently. "I'm sorry."

"What good's sorry now that you got what you wanted?" Jamie demanded, not the least bit pacified by the apology.

"He's gonna get us riding lessons," Josh said so softly it was barely audible.

Jamie gaped. "That was the deal? You traded our secret for riding lessons?"

"I know how bad you wanted them," Josh said defensively. "I did it for you."

"He did," Michael said. "And I'll get somebody over here this afternoon."

"Yeah," Jamie said bitterly. "And right after that, you'll turn us in."

"Nobody's turning anybody in," Grace assured him. "This just makes it easier for me to get information." She regarded Jamie evenly. "I'm a lawyer and I am on your side."

Jamie continued to regard her with suspicion. "We can't afford to pay a lawyer."

Grace returned his look with a solemn expression. "Do you have any money at all?"

"A couple of dollars," Jamie said.

Josh looked surprised. "You said we was broke."

"This was for emergencies," Jamie said defensively.

"Give me one of the dollars," Grace said.

Jamie balked. "What about the emergencies?"

"Once you give me that dollar, I'll be working for you. I'll take care of any emergencies," she explained.

Jamie still looked dubious. "Honest?"

"Honest."

He took a crumpled bill from his pocket and handed it to her. Grace smoothed it out, folded it and put it in her pocket.

"Now you have yourself a lawyer," she said. "With me on your side, nothing will happen to the two of you unless we all agree it's for the best."

"All of us?" Jamie repeated skeptically. "That means me and Josh have to say yes, too?"

"Absolutely," she assured him.

Michael regarded her with surprise. Surely she knew that making such a promise was risky. What if the court overruled their judgment? Just as Jamie had said earlier, grown-ups in general and judges in particular could be notoriously capricious, even in interpreting the letter of the law.

Jamie seemed to be wavering, his distrust of the system weighing heavily against his longing to ride one of the horses.

"Do I get to pick which horse?" he asked.

"As long as whoever comes to give the lesson approves it," Michael said. When Jamie looked ready to protest, he added, "Just to make sure you won't get hurt. Once you've had your lessons, you can ride any horse around here."

"Satisfied?" Grace asked.

Josh stared up at his big brother hopefully. "Is it okay?"

Jamie shuffled his sneakers in the dirt, trying very hard to bank his obvious excitement. "I suppose."

"All right!" Josh shouted, slapping Michael's hand in a high five.

Michael had to admit, he felt a little of the child's glee himself. A glance at Grace suggested she was just as happy. A smile had spread across her face and lit her eyes. Only Jamie refused to give any outward hint of his exuberance. All alone, he headed back into the barn. After a slight hesitation, Josh trailed after him.

"I guess you're pretty proud that your divide-and-conquer technique paid off," Grace said, a surprising hint of condemnation in her voice.

"I'm glad we have the information we need," he agreed. He met her gaze evenly. "But I wish there had been another way to get it. I don't want those boys to lose their trust in one another."

She regarded him with obvious relief. "Good. Then you won't try that again."

"Since you obviously disapprove of my methods, does that mean you don't want the ill-gotten information?"

"No," she said quickly. "Of course, I want it."

"The last name is Miller. The mother is Naomi. Any luck with your other calls?"

"Nothing so far, but it's hard to get a line on something like this without giving away more than I'm getting. It'll be easier now that I'm not just trying to track down two needles in a very large haystack."

Michael regarded her worriedly. "Grace, how much trouble will you be in if someone wants to make a big deal out of the two of us letting those kids stay here instead of turning them in right away? I imagine there are pretty strict regulations governing this sort of thing. We can't just decide to keep the kids here without somebody's approval, right? Not even for a few days?"

"I can handle it. What about you? If some newspaper gets wind of your involvement, this could land on the front pages of the papers all over Texas."

"I've weathered worse," he assured her. It came with the territory. There were a lot of people eager to dig up dirt on a family as powerful as the Delacourts. There wasn't much to be found, but a lot could be made of a little indiscretion if a reporter cared to put a negative slant on it.

"All that matters is getting those boys settled someplace where they'll be together and happy," he told her.

She smiled up at him then, one of those bright, sunny smiles that held nothing back. Drawn to her, he slipped closer, and before she could realize his intention, he leaned down and touched his lips lightly to hers. Silken heat, whisper-soft against his, her mouth was every bit as wickedly tempting as he'd recalled. He had to force himself to stop at just one kiss.

"Thank you for coming to their defense," he whispered against her cheek.

She gazed up at him, her lips parted in astonishment.

His resolve fled. The first kiss had felt so good and her mouth was so thoroughly tempting that Michael couldn't resist one more taste. This time when his mouth slanted across hers, a deep sigh shuddered through her and was echoed in his body.

How was it possible after all these years apart, after all of their legal skirmishes, that something as simple as a kiss felt like coming home? Now that he knew that, he could hardly wait to get Jamie and Josh's situation settled, so that he and Grace could start over.

If she'd agree.

## Chapter Five

Dazed by the unexpected kiss and even more stunned by her response to it, Grace stared at Michael. "What was that all about?"

"Just a little thank-you kiss," he assured her, but his lips were curved into a satisfied smile.

"The first one, maybe," she said, resisting the desire to touch her fingers to her still-tingling mouth. "That second one was something else altogether."

"Was it really?" he asked innocently. "It got to you, did it?"

The man was infuriating. Smug.

Accurate, she thought with a barely concealed sigh. It would not do to let him see it, though. "It did not *get to me,* as you put it," she said staunchly. "I am immune to you, Michael Delacourt. I have been for years."

"Then the kiss meant nothing, did it? It's hardly worth all this analysis."

"That's exactly right. It meant absolutely nothing!" She whirled around and headed for the house, fully aware of his faint chuckle trailing after her.

Oh, yes, the man was impossible. He was trying to start something, either to satisfy his ego that he could still make it happen or because he was bored and she was conveniently available as a distraction. As if two runaway kids weren't enough trouble, he was looking for more.

Coming here was a mistake, she told herself as she went into the kitchen and splashed cold water on her flushed cheeks, then stood still and fought to quiet the racing of her pulse.

No, she corrected, staying was the mistake. She should have turned right around the night before and gone back to Houston. She could have driven the rental car all the way, if need be, taking Jamie and Josh with her. Of course, they might well have ended up in New Mexico if she'd tried, but that would have been better than this off-kilter way she was feeling right this second.

Even before she heard Michael's booted footsteps on the porch, she sensed that he was near. She could feel a vague and once all-too-familiar prickling sensation on the back of her neck, the same sensation that warned of danger closing in. She quickly dried her cheeks and turned to face him with what she hoped was a totally calm, disinterested expression. She'd had plenty of time to perfect it over the years. Every time they met, in fact.

"Feeling in control again?" he inquired with amusement flashing in his eyes.

"You really do have an overinflated ego," she pointed out.

"I find confidence to be necessary in business."

"Confidence and ego are not exactly the same," she remarked tartly.

He wasn't put off in the least. In fact, he seemed to be enjoying the debate, deliberately prolonging it. "I suppose that depends on how you define them."

"Confidence has to do with knowing your own strengths. Ego has to do with overinflating them, giving yourself a little too much credit." She leveled a haughty look straight at him. "It is not an attractive quality."

"Then just think of the fun you can have over the next few days trying to cut my overinflated ego back down to size," he suggested.

"I am not here for your personal amusement or my own," she pointed out huffily. "The only reason I agreed to stay was because of Jamie and Josh."

Michael nodded. "Of course," he intoned solemnly. "I'll try to remember that."

She drew herself up and leveled a stern look straight at him. It usually worked quite well on a reluctant witness. "See that you do."

She had no earthly idea why her words seemed to make him smile, but she caught him doing just that, even though he quickly hid it. She decided it was wisest to let the matter drop. It was evident she wasn't winning the debate, couldn't against a man who didn't play by any rules and didn't seem the least bit wary of the outcome.

"I'd better make those calls," she said. "Is there another phone around here that's more private? I don't want Jamie or Josh to come in and overhear me."

"There's one in the den," he said, leading her toward a small but airy room that faced the sun-splashed fields of wildflowers at the back of the house. French doors opened onto a deck and let in the rapidly warming morning breeze.

While there was a masculine feel to much of the house, this room had been designed for a woman. The view had been brought indoors with splashes of brightly colored chintz on the sofa and a collection of chintz-patterned teacups on an old oak sideboard. The furniture was scaled-down in size, too, comfortable, but far more feminine than the oversized, darkly upholstered chairs in the living room. Books, some of them lying open as if abandoned in midsentence, were scattered everywhere and ranged in topic from the latest fiction to a colorful book on quilts as art.

Grace instantly fell in love with all of it. It was thoroughly charming and such a stark contrast to the tidy, practical, modern decor in her Houston condo, where a weekly maid chased away dust and disorder.

"What a wonderful room," she said, circling it to admire the lush combination of fabrics, the eclectic touches that hinted of Trish's various interests. This had to be her special domain, a home office, perhaps.

"Trish's haven, as I understand it," Michael said, confirming her guess. "Hardy custom-built all the bookshelves and cabinets."

"They're beautiful," Grace said, thinking that they, like the rest of the house he'd built, had been imbued with such care and love. "Your sister is a very lucky woman."

"I think she'd agree with you." He stood there uncertainly for a moment, his gaze skimming hers. "Well, I guess I'll leave you to make those calls. I'd better make a few of my own. I have to track down a riding instructor."

"Do you need to use the phone first?"

"I'll use my cell phone." He grinned. "I hid it in my briefcase in case my family got any crazy ideas about cutting off the phone service on me."

She regarded him with a sudden burst of insight. "You know something, Michael? I think you're almost disappointed that they didn't."

"Why on earth would you say that? I hated that last vacation."

"But you liked the fact that they cared enough to make you go, didn't you?"

He seemed startled by the observation, but then he nodded slowly. "You know, you may be right. I suppose we all want someone who'll look out for our best interests when we forget to." He studied her with quiet intensity. "Do you have someone who does that for you, Grace?"

"Sure," she said blithely, hoping he would let it go at that. But of course, being Michael, he didn't.

"Who?"

"That's my private business," she told him stiffly, because there was no way on earth that she would admit that *she* was the only person who looked out for Grace Foster. She watched herself intently for signs of burnout, scheduled vacations that took her far from Houston where no one could reach her, vacations during which she went almost as nuts as she supposed Michael did.

"Well, I just hope whoever it is does the job right," he said softly. Then he turned and left her alone.

Grace sighed. Why was it that holed up here in Los Piños with Michael and two young boys—more people than she ever had crowded around—she suddenly felt more lonely than ever?

Before she could ponder that for too long, the phone rang. Hoping that it was a reply to one of her earlier inquiries, she snatched it up on the first ring.

"Well, well, well," a teasing masculine voice said. "Who is this?"

Grace stiffened. "Who is *this?*" she shot right back, not prepared to give anything away.

"Tyler Delacourt," he said at once.

Her shoulders relaxed. She had always liked the most charming of the Delacourt brothers. He had a twinkle in his eyes, a flirtatious nature and a heart as big as Texas. While others in the family had never warmed to her, Tyler had. He'd always treated her as if they were coconspirators in the battle to hold on to Michael's heart.

"Tyler, I didn't recognize your voice," she said, aware of just how much she'd missed him, right along with his brother. Breaking up with Michael had meant losing his whole family, a family she had come to think of as her own, even if they hadn't seen it quite that way. It would have been awkward, though, and far too painful, to stay in touch even with Tyler, so she hadn't. "This is Grace."

"Grace Foster?" Tyler asked.

He sounded a little shocked, but just as delighted as she was. She had to wonder, though, if it was for the same reason. Tyler had done his best to help Michael mend fences with her all those years ago. He'd considered it a personal failure that he hadn't succeeded.

"Oh, my, how did my brother manage to lure you over to his vacation hideaway?" he said.

His amused tone confirmed her fear that he'd leaped to the wrong conclusion. "Don't make too much of it," she warned.

"How can I not? I thought you two weren't on speaking terms."

"We speak," Grace said, then grinned as she thought of the last conversation she and Michael had had during the debacle between Delacourt Oil and Brianna O'Rourke, who was now Mrs. Jeb Delacourt. "To be more precise, we usually shout."

"Is there a lot of shouting going on now?" Tyler inquired with unabashed curiosity. "Did I interrupt?"

"Nope. All's quiet on the western front. Since you obviously called to speak to your brother, why don't I get him for you?"

"Wait," he commanded.

"Yes?"

"Whatever the reason for it, I'm glad you're there," he said quietly.

Grace was startled by his unexpectedly serious tone. "Why would my being here matter to you?"

He hesitated, then said, "It just does, okay? Give him a chance, Grace. Michael's missed you, more than he'll probably ever admit, even to himself. He needs you in his life.''

It was a familiar refrain, but she didn't believe it for a second, couldn't allow herself to believe it. "Tyler, don't get the wrong idea. My reason for being here isn't personal. This isn't about Michael and me. Let me get him. I'm sure he'll explain.''

Taking the portable phone with her, she went in search of Michael and found him on the outside deck, legs stretched out in front of him, face turned up to the sun, eyes closed. For a man who professed not to know how to relax, he seemed to have found a way.

"Michael?" she said softly, not sure if he'd drifted off to sleep.

He snagged her hand, proving that he'd been aware of her presence all along. "Come sit with me," he said without opening his eyes.

"Not just now," she said, easing out of his grip. "Your brother's on the phone."

His eyes snapped open then. "Which one?" he mouthed silently.

"Tyler."

"Oh, boy," he muttered, taking the phone. "Hey, Ty, what's up?"

Grace turned to leave, but paused when she heard his low chuckle.

"Stay out of it, bro. You dumped me over here without a second thought. Now it's up to me how I occupy my time."

Obviously she hadn't been convincing enough during her own conversation with Tyler. He clearly wasn't buying the fact that her presence here wasn't personal. She had to wonder why. Was she a frequent topic of conversation between the brothers? What sort of speculation had Tyler engaged in over the years? He seemed to think she really mattered to Michael, when she knew the opposite was true. But which of them knew Michael best? Once she would have said she did, but after all this time, maybe Tyler did have more insight.

Oh, what did it matter? she asked herself impatiently. Whatever regrets she or Michael had, it was impossible to recapture the past.

Even so, she found herself moving deliberately right back into Michael's line of vision to wait for the return of the phone. Maybe that way she could inhibit whatever he might otherwise be inclined to say about her easy agreement to his request that she fly over. After that earlier taunt about her eagerness to get him out of his clothes—after that kiss—it was clear that Michael wasn't solely focused on her ability to help Josh and Jamie. That didn't mean the whole family had to start leaping to conclusions.

After a surprisingly brief exchange, Michael hung up and handed her the phone.

"Tyler said to tell you goodbye."

"It was nice to speak to him," she said honestly.

"He always thought you hung the moon," Michael told her. "Said I was a damned fool for letting you get away."

This was not a conversation she intended to have. "You were," she said simply, then turned and went back inside, fully aware with every step she took that Michael's startled, intense gaze was following her.

\* \* \*

Grace managed to stay out of Michael's path for the next few hours. She fixed sandwiches, then left them in the refrigerator for Jamie, Josh and Michael, before taking her own lunch and retreating to the den, where she firmly closed the door to prevent intrusions. She barely resisted the urge to lock it.

It was nearly three o'clock before she finally put the phone back on the hook, then uttered a heartfelt sigh. She shrugged her shoulders trying to work out the knots of tension.

The calls had gone about as she'd expected. She'd received a flurry of faxes indicating just how troublesome Jamie and Josh Miller had been to their various foster families and just how far Naomi Miller was from being fully recovered from her addiction. There was a lot of frustration from social services, who had about given up on finding anyplace where the boys would stay put, much less thrive.

"Why the interest?" a friend in the Houston department had asked her. Shirley Lee Green—mother of four and foster mom to a dozen more over the years—had agreed to make a few inquiries on Grace's behalf. "Those two are on the other side of the state, out of our jurisdiction. At the moment, they're missing." She paused, then asked suspiciously, "You haven't had any contact with them, have you?"

"I can't answer that," Grace said.

"Oh, baby, don't go getting involved in something like this," Shirley Lee had declared, correctly reading her avoidance of the question as assent. "I know you. You'll get your heart broken."

"Thanks for making the calls," Grace said, ignoring the well-intentioned advice from a very good friend, who also happened to be the best advocate she knew for troubled kids. "You're an angel."

"What I am is one worried mama," Shirley Lee retorted. "You know I look on you as one of my own flock. I don't want you getting yourself hurt. You're one of the last good guys."

That assessment was still ringing in her ears when she heard the squeals of delight from outside, then Michael's shouted warning and the softer, more patient voice of another man. Apparently the riding lesson had commenced. Because the last few hours had been so thoroughly frustrating, she couldn't resist the chance to peek outside and see Josh and Jamie engaged in something that obviously made them happy.

What she didn't expect to find was Michael sitting uncomfortably in a saddle, while two upturned faces regarded him with apparent glee. Josh caught sight of her first.

"Hey, Grace, Michael almost fell off the horse," he shouted. "Me and Jamie didn't. Slade says we're real naturals, didn't you, Slade?"

A lanky cowboy turned toward her and tipped his hat. "Ma'am."

"Hi, I'm Grace Foster," she said.

"Slade Sutton. I work over at White Pines. Harlan Adams sent me over to see if I could turn these three into cowboys." He winked at the boys. "I'm doing right well with these two." He gave a nod in Michael's direction. "He's another story. Doesn't trust the horse."

"He's a business tycoon," Grace confided. "He doesn't trust anything."

Slade grinned. "Ah, that explains it. Think he'd do better with a pretty little filly?"

Grace stole a quick look at Michael and discovered he was taking the teasing in stride. "Oh, he'd like a filly, all right, but he still wouldn't trust her."

"Okay, you guys, that's enough." Michael swung his leg over the horse and dismounted, fairly smoothly in Grace's opinion. She had to wonder if some of his awkwardness hadn't been for Josh and Jamie's benefit, to give them a much needed sense of being better than an adult at something.

He stalked straight to Grace, put his hands on her waist and hoisted her into the saddle before she could catch her breath to protest. "How does it feel up there?" he inquired, regarding her with amusement.

Because she wasn't about to give him the satisfaction of begging to be rescued, she settled herself more securely in the saddle and gave the question some real thought. "Interesting," she said at last. "I like the vantage point. It's not often I get to look down on a couple of tall men."

"Teach her, too," the boys begged Slade.

The cowboy looked up at her. "You care for a little spin around the corral?"

"Why not?" she said gamely.

He led the horse around in a big circle until she got the feel of being in the saddle.

"Ready to try it on your own?"

"Sure." She listened carefully to his instructions, then followed them precisely. She was pleased—and more than a little relieved—when the horse obeyed her commands.

"Another natural," Slade commended her, helping her down at the end of the lesson.

"Can we ride again?" Jamie asked, regarding the horse with longing.

"Not today," Michael said. "We have to let Slade get back to his job."

"I'll be back around this time tomorrow," Slade promised.

The boys turned fearfully toward Grace, all of the animation drained out of their faces.

"Will we still be here?" Josh asked, a telltale quiver in his voice.

"You'll be here," Grace assured him. She and Michael had some serious decisions to make tonight, but in the meantime, the one thing she knew with absolute certainty was that Jamie and Josh weren't going anywhere. Not yet.

Unaware of the undercurrents, Slade merely nodded. "Then I'll see you tomorrow."

Michael walked with him toward his pickup, leaving Grace alone with the boys. Eyes shining again, Josh immediately started in with a blow-by-blow account of their riding lesson.

"It was so cool," he concluded. "It was the very best thing we ever got to do."

Grace smiled at his exuberance, but she couldn't help noticing that Jamie hadn't said a word. "Jamie, was it everything you expected it to be, too?"

He lifted his too-serious gaze to meet hers. "Nobody has ever done anything like this for us before. No matter what you guys do with us, we won't ever forget that you were real nice to us."

She thought she saw him blink back tears before

he turned and ran off to the barn, Josh hard on his
heels.

"Jamie, what's wrong?" Josh called out worriedly. "Jamie?"

Grace couldn't hear the boy's mumbled response,
couldn't swear that she heard him fighting to choke
back a sob, but she took a step after him just the
same, then stopped herself. Jamie wouldn't welcome
her sympathy. The only thing that would really matter to him was her ability to find some way to guarantee them a better future. How in heaven's name
was she supposed to do that when an overburdened
social services system was just waiting to swallow
them up again?

## Chapter Six

After a full day of sun and exercise, both Jamie and Josh were exhausted. To Michael's astonishment, right after an early dinner, they agreed without protest to go upstairs to take baths and go to bed.

They were almost out the kitchen door when Josh turned and ran back to enfold Grace in a hug. Clearly startled by the gesture, she stood totally still for an instant before allowing her hand to come to rest on the boy's head.

Michael watched the play of emotions on her face—surprise, sorrow, yearning—and wondered for the first time if he had dragged her into the middle of something that she wasn't emotionally equipped to handle. As usual, he'd selfishly thought only of his own desperation when he'd called her. He hadn't stopped for a second to consider what becoming involved with the boys might do to Grace.

Despite her tough demeanor as a lawyer, he knew better than anyone how tenderhearted Grace really was, how easily bruised her feelings could be. He also knew just how badly she had once wanted a family of her own, how much she had envied him his large collection of relatives. When she had willingly sacrificed all of that to cut him out of her life, he had finally realized just how deeply he had hurt her.

Worried by the strain he thought he detected, he watched her intently.

Finally, after some sort of internal struggle, she forced a smile for Josh and said in her usual bright manner, "Off with you. Lights out in half an hour, okay?"

"Could you maybe come up and tuck us in?" Josh asked hopefully.

"Aw, come on, Josh, we're not babies," Jamie protested. He had remained hovering in the doorway. From his expression it was evident he longed to be where Josh was, but it was just as clear he thought himself too old for such an overt demonstration of affection.

Grace seemed to sense his longing, too. "You may be too big for me to tuck you in, but I'll come up anyway," Grace promised, then grinned. "So be sure to wash behind your ears, guys. I'll check."

Jamie's expression brightened at the teasing. He was clearly relieved to have found a way to be included without giving up his adolescent dignity.

"You'll have to catch me first," he retorted.

"You'd be surprised how quick I am when I'm motivated," Grace warned him.

After the boys had gone, she leaned against the counter and sighed.

"Grace?" Michael asked. "You okay?"

She frowned at the question. "Would you stop asking me that? I'm fine."

"Are you sure you're not in over your head? If you are, it's my fault and we need to move ahead with this, get it over with."

"We're not going to rush it. My involvement is not your fault," she said, avoiding the thrust of his question. "I'm here of my own free will."

"You're here because I called."

"Michael, don't make a big deal out of it," she said with a trace of impatience. "I'm a lawyer. This is what I do."

"No. This is above and beyond what you normally do," he corrected. "You're living under the same roof with Jamie and Josh. You're seeing on a minute-by-minute basis how deeply they've been hurt in the past. You're seeing how badly they crave attention and love. It's tearing you apart, isn't it?"

"I'll survive," she insisted, her gaze daring him to contradict her or to prolong the discussion.

"I think we need to put a stop to it. Let someone else take over."

"Absolutely not," she said fiercely. Her gaze clashed with his. "If you do that, Michael, I will never forgive you."

Michael knew enough to let it go. It wouldn't help if he became any more a part of the problem than he already was.

"Okay, then. We'll leave things as they are for the time being. Are you ready to talk about what you found out today?" he asked instead.

"Not just yet," she said, her attention seemingly riveted on the dishes in the sink. "Why don't you go on out to the deck? I'll join you after I've finished here and said good-night to Jamie and Josh."

He nodded, sensing that she needed the time alone to gather her composure. Because he couldn't think of any other way to help her, he gave her shoulder a light squeeze, took his glass of wine and went outside.

That didn't mean he could shake the vision of the strongest woman he knew looking as if she wanted desperately to cry. Worse, no matter what she said, he knew he was the one responsible for turning her heart inside out yet another time. What he didn't know was how to make any of it right...or precisely why he wanted to so badly.

Grace didn't know how to cope with being needed. Oh, sure, her clients needed her. They came to her during an emotional crisis in their lives, but what they needed was legal advice, an advocate in the courtroom, someone impartial who would stand up for them against injustice. They needed Grace Foster, Attorney-at-Law, not Grace Foster the woman.

Jamie and Josh were different. While Michael might have turned to her for her legal expertise, the boys needed something else. They needed someone to care about them, someone they could love and trust.

Josh, still an innocent at eight, was already turning

to her for that. Jamie—older, wiser, less trusting—
was more cautious. It was as if he recognized that
she might like them, but that she was also in a position to turn their lives upside down again. She
didn't know how to risk giving them what they
needed without setting them up for another possible
disappointment. All she could do was play it by ear,
one second at a time. She would not allow Michael
to interfere in that. He'd brought her over here. He
would just have to accept her decisions.

The boys had already fallen asleep by the time she
finished the dishes and climbed the stairs. She leaned
down and pressed a light kiss to Josh's cheek, then
stood staring down at Jamie. His blond cowlick was
standing up, but his face was more at peace than
usual. Long lashes were smudges against his pale
cheeks. She smiled at those dark lashes. He was going to be a heartbreaker one day soon. He would
grow up, flesh out his lanky frame with muscle, and
bestow that rare, dimpled smile of his on some girl
who'd fall in love just at the sight of it. Grace had
the feeling that whatever happened in the next few
days would make all the difference in whether Jamie
accepted that love or turned away.

"Sweet dreams," she whispered to him, brushing
a gentle hand over his mussed hair.

As if he heard her, he mumbled something in his
sleep, then shifted restlessly away from her touch.
Grace sighed.

After casting one last look at the Miller brothers,
she switched off the overhead light and left the room.
Now she just had to go back downstairs and face
Michael.

What was she going to say to him? After their earlier conversation how could she tell him that she had no intention of calling anyone, not tonight certainly and maybe not even tomorrow, although she knew the time had come to advise the authorities that Jamie and Josh Miller had been found? Michael would be appalled, not only by her lapse of ethics, but by what it said about her emotional involvement. He already suspected she was in too deep.

Desperate to avoid a conflict with him, she sorted through every alternative she could think of. Maybe she could legitimately buy the boys another day or two here with them through some fancy legal footwork, but after that there would be no choice, she finally concluded with a sigh. Unless she and Michael could come up with another alternative, the boys would have to go back into the foster care system.

Realistically, they would probably be separated again, too. The thought of it broke her heart. She couldn't let that happen. She just couldn't.

In order to forestall the inevitable, she would just have to stretch the truth to suit her purposes. If Michael so much as suspected that it was only a matter of time before social services traced the boys' whereabouts, thanks to her inquiries, he would insist on meeting the issue head-on. It wasn't that he was heartless, just pragmatic. He would insist that a clean, quick break was the right thing for everyone.

Everyone except Josh and Jamie, she thought heatedly. They needed more time together. They deserved it. No matter what happened afterward, she could give them that.

Outside on the deck, there was a gentle spring breeze, scented with roses. Michael looked up when she walked outside.

"The boys asleep?"

"They were sound asleep before I even got upstairs," she said with a smile. "All the fresh air and riding obviously exhausted them. Thank you for arranging the lesson for them."

"It was nothing," he said.

"Not to them. It meant the world to them. They told me no one had ever done anything like that for them before. It's very sad, really. It would take so little to make them really happy."

"I've been thinking," Michael said. "For kids who've been bounced around the way they have, they haven't turned out too badly. Other than running away, I don't see any sign that they're bad kids. Jamie defies authority, but what kid his age doesn't, and he has more reason than most. Why can't the foster parents see that?"

"He may not be giving them a chance," Grace suggested. "He may be so focused on getting back to Josh that he does whatever he can to avoid getting attached. I've known foster kids who always kept their suitcases packed because they just assumed they would eventually get sent away again."

"It's no way for a kid to live," Michael said with surprising passion.

"No, it isn't."

He glanced over at her. "What did you find out today?"

She decided to stick as closely as she could to the truth, as long as she could do it without raising any red flags. "Nothing we didn't already know. They're regarded as problem kids."

"Is anyone looking for them?"

"The appropriate authorities were notified when they disappeared. The police are supposed to be looking out for them."

Michael shook his head. "I meant does anyone actually give a damn that they're missing?"

The vehemence of his question startled her. He sounded angry on Josh and Jamie's behalf. Because he did, she answered candidly. "No. Not the way you mean. The foster parents are more frustrated than worried. I'm sure there are social services people who are good-hearted and who might be worried, but their caseloads are piled high. Jamie and Josh are just two more kids vying for attention on their radar. Runaways are a tragic fact of life."

"Damn," Michael muttered. "So, what do we do next? Call up and relieve their minds, tell them that the boys are safe?"

"If we do, they'll insist on picking them up," Grace warned.

"And if we don't?"

"The boys will have a little more time together." She regarded Michael anxiously. "Would that be so terrible?"

He sighed heavily. "Grace, I can see a thousand and one pitfalls to what you're suggesting."

"So can I," she conceded. "I'm not blind, Michael, or stupid. I'm aware of the risks."

"But you want to take them anyway," he said.

"A few days," she said again. "It seems like the least we can do. You're here. I'm here. We're both responsible. If anyone goes crazy, we have the clout to make them see that this was just a gift we were giving Jamie and Josh. What possible harm can come of it?''

Michael shook his head, regarding her worriedly. ''It's a gift that could seriously backfire on all of us. You could lose your license to practice law, couldn't you? You're interfering in a court-ordered process. Even with the best motives in the world, keeping them here is wrong.''

''I'm willing to chance it,'' she said defiantly. ''If you're worried about your reputation, I'll take the boys and we'll leave here.''

He scowled at her. ''Don't be ridiculous. I'm not worried about myself. I'm concerned about you and I'm concerned about Josh and Jamie. They're already attached to you. What will happen after a few more days?''

She felt his gaze searching hers.

''And how will you feel when you have to stand by and watch them go?'' he asked quietly.

Grace swallowed hard. ''It will tear me apart,'' she said honestly. ''But it would tear me apart now. A few more days won't make that much difference. Besides, in the meantime maybe we'll come up with a better solution.''

Michael's brow was still knit with concern. ''I don't know.''

''I'm not asking, Michael,'' she said finally. ''I'm telling you that this is how it's going to be. The only question is whether we stay here with you or I take them back to Houston.''

He seemed taken aback by her defiant tone, but

then a grin spread slowly across his face. "Stay here, by all means. When the trouble hits the fan, you're going to need somebody to stand up and fight for you."

"And you'll do that?" she asked skeptically.

"Of course."

"Why, Michael? You could be rid of all of us, wash your hands of this little inconvenience. That's what you intended when you first called me."

"Maybe so," he agreed. "But those kids have grown on me, too. Besides, you're here now, back to being a thorn in my side again. I guess a part of me missed that more than I'd realized."

The admission, even phrased as it was, sent a shiver through her. She'd missed it, too. No one had ever challenged her mentally the way Michael did. No one made her feel as much like a woman as he did. She drew in a deep breath and reminded herself that feeling that way was a luxury she couldn't afford right now, not with the fate of Jamie and Josh at stake.

"It isn't personal," she reminded him, wanting to make that very clear.

"Of course not."

"I mean it, Michael."

"If you'd come over here, I'll bet I could prove otherwise," he taunted.

Because she knew he was right, she stayed right where she was. "Not in a million years," she declared.

"Chicken."

"Prudent," she countered.

He laughed. "That's okay. I've just bought myself

a little more time to see if I can persuade you to change your mind. I've always loved a challenge, Grace. Surely you remember that.''

She did. That, and so much more that it scared the living daylights out of her. For reasons she didn't care to explore too closely, she still couldn't help being glad that he wasn't sending them on their way.

By morning Grace still felt as if she and the boys had been granted a reprieve, even if it had come from Michael and not the proper authorities. As she listened to Josh and Jamie's excited chatter about their next riding lesson and their plans to explore the rest of the ranch—and to Michael chiming in with an offer to accompany them—she felt an amazing sense of peace steal over her. There was something so right about this, something that felt good deep inside.

"Well, while you all are out having your male adventure, I have a few plans of my own," she announced.

Three pairs of eyes turned to her. Michael's and Josh's were alight with curiosity. Jamie's were wary.

"Like what?" he asked.

She winked at him, hoping to wipe that worried look off of his face. "It's a surprise."

"No way," he protested, sounding almost panicky. "You gotta tell."

"Then it wouldn't be a surprise," she said. "It's a good surprise, Jamie. I promise. Now, go on. Get ready to go exploring. I'll even pack you all a picnic lunch."

Jamie cast one last worried look in her direction

before eventually following Josh upstairs. That left Michael watching her intently.

"What do you have up your sleeve?"

"You'll see."

"You don't intend to tell me, either?"

"You might blab."

"I am the very soul of discretion, I'll have you know. Nothing gets past my lips, unless I want it to."

"Once two people know a secret, it's not a secret anymore," she insisted.

"I take it you think I'll approve."

"I know you will." She hesitated, then admitted, "There is one thing that concerns me, though."

"What's that?"

"I'll have to go into town to pull this off."

"Not a problem. You have the rental car."

"Easy for you to say," she muttered, then reminded him, "I have no idea where town is."

He chuckled then. "And even if you did, there's no guarantee you'd know how to find it."

"Very amusing. Can you just draw me a map? I'm very good if I have a precise map."

"I thought my pilot gave you a map the other night."

She waved off the reminder. "He gave me directions. That's not the same at all."

"Maybe we should all go into town."

"Oh, no, you don't. That would ruin everything. Just draw me a map."

Michael uttered a resigned sigh, grabbed a piece of paper and drew her a very detailed map, then went over it with her as carefully as if a wrong turn might lead her into a minefield.

"Got it?" he asked.

"That should get me there," she agreed.

"Maybe you should scatter breadcrumbs behind you, so you can find your way back."

"Not a problem," she assured him, waving the piece of paper. "I just reverse these."

"How long should I wait before I send out a search party?" he teased.

"If I'm not back by dinnertime, forget the search party. Just give me a call in Houston. I could decide that you're more trouble than you're worth and hightail it out of here."

"Not a chance. You might abandon me, but you wouldn't desert Josh and Jamie."

Unfortunately, he had that pegged exactly right. Rather than admit it, she grabbed her purse and car keys off the counter and headed for the door.

"I'll see you later."

"You sound so sure of that," he noted with amusement. "Must be my outstanding directions. They've given you confidence."

She waved them at him. "They'd better be fool-proof," she warned him.

"Oh, they are, darlin'. I want you back here too much to take any chances."

There was a heartfelt note in his voice that she was pretty sure didn't have anything to do with wanting her here for Josh and Jamie's sakes. It left her feeling warm all over in a way that was definitely dangerous. Michael was right about the pitfalls of these stolen days extending to the two of them.

She pushed that troublesome worry out of her head to concentrate on Michael's very precise directions. She was determined not to get herself lost.

When she finally pulled into a parking place in front of Dolan's, she uttered a fervent sigh of relief. Noticing that the drugstore had a lunch counter, she decided to treat herself to a soda while she asked advice about stores and planned out her shopping.

At midmorning, the counter was deserted. The woman behind it was trying to soothe a cranky toddler, who was clearly unhappy about being restricted to a playpen. When she turned to greet Grace, the child let out a wail.

"It's not a good day," the woman said, plucking the toddler up and settling her in her arms. "I don't understand it. This is my third. The first two loved being here all day long, getting showered with attention. This one isn't happy unless she's running up and down the aisles pulling all the stock off the shelves."

"I guess all kids are different," Grace said. "You just have to adapt."

"Or go crazy," the woman agreed. "I'm Sharon Lynn, by the way. Are you new in town?"

"Actually, I'm visiting." She considered how to explain the exact circumstances. "I'm staying with someone who came here to visit his sister."

Sharon Lynn's expression brightened. "Ah, Trish's brother, I'll bet. I'd heard they were trying to get him away from his office."

"You know Trish?"

"Sure. Her bookstore's right next door. Of course, it's closed this week because she and Hardy went out of town to give Michael the peace and quiet they thought he needed." She chuckled as if she were in on the joke. "How's he taking it?"

"Probably a lot better than they imagined when they took off on him, but I don't think it's quite as peaceful or quiet as anyone expected."

Sharon Lynn chuckled. "No, I imagine you being here definitely changed the game plan. They didn't mention he'd be bringing a friend."

"Oh, I'm not a friend," Grace protested hurriedly. "Not the way you mean. I came on a mission of mercy." Though she had warmed to Sharon Lynn immediately, she hesitated to say more. The fewer people who knew the whole story about the boys, the better.

"Sounds fascinating. Tell me what I can get for you and you can tell me all about it."

"Just a soda," Grace said. "And I've probably already said too much. You can help me with something, though. I need to do a little shopping for groceries and for a few birthday presents. Can you steer me in the right direction?"

"You're on Main Street. This is our shopping district, so you can't very well get lost."

"That's a relief," Grace murmured.

"What?"

"I'm not so hot with directions. Some consider it a character flaw."

"I say you're either born with a sense of direction or you're not. Blame it on genetics," Sharon Lynn advised. "What sort of gifts are you looking for?"

"For a boy who just turned eight. I'm not even

sure what a kid that age is interested in. This one loves horses, but beyond that, I don't know.''

"Then he's not yours," Sharon Lynn concluded. "A nephew?"

"No."

Sharon Lynn's penetrating gaze studied her. "And that's all you intend to say, isn't it?"

"Pretty much. Sorry."

"Don't worry about it. If you're around here long, you'll discover that the Adamses are notoriously nosy. You'll also learn when to tell us to take a hike."

"Ah, the Adamses," she repeated slowly. "And you're Sharon Lynn. I should have put two and two together. I've heard of you."

"Through Trish's brother?"

"Actually no, I read about your custody case when I was researching family law."

The case had fascinated her even then, an intriguing story of a baby left on the doorstep of this very store and Sharon Lynn's fight to keep her. How much of that case might prove to be relevant to the situation in which she and Michael had found themselves? And wasn't it her step-grandmother, the legendary Janet Runningbear Adams, who had fought the case and won?

"You're a lawyer?" Sharon Lynn asked, regarding her with surprise.

Grace nodded. "In Houston."

"And that's how you know Michael?"

Grace laughed. "You're good, you know that? Another few minutes, you'd have my entire life history. It's a darn good thing I have to get this shopping done.''

''It won't take long. It's not a big town. Stop back for lunch.''

''I'll think about it. If I don't get back by, it was very nice meeting you, Sharon Lynn.''

''You, too. I hope I'll see you again while you're here.''

Grace slipped out of the drugstore before Sharon Lynn could do any more of her innocent prying. She paused outside Trish's bookstore and peered in the window. She could see the same cozy atmosphere in there that Trish had created in her home.

Across the street she found the baking supplies she needed at the general store, then moved on to the other shops looking for inspiration. When she found the cowboy boots, she knew she'd hit pay dirt. She had to guess at Josh's size, but the proprietor assured her she could bring them back if they didn't fit. She added some more western attire, including a pint-sized Stetson, had it all boxed up and put it in the back of her car.

By then it was lunchtime, so she decided to take Sharon Lynn up on her invitation, but she couldn't help being relieved that it was too busy for another interrogation. She bought wrapping paper and balloons before leaving the drugstore, then headed back to the ranch.

She actually made the trip without mishap, not even a single wrong turn. She was back at the house before the guys returned from their adventure, though she beat them by only a few minutes. They came in bursting with excitement, Josh's words tumbling over each other as he told her about their morning. Jamie's exuberance was more restrained, but his expression was equally happy. And both of them kept turning to Michael for approval. Obviously he was rapidly becoming the male role model they both desperately needed.

Michael met her gaze over the boys' heads. "Home safe and sound, I see."

"I told you I would be."

He glanced around the kitchen. "Where's the surprise?"

He sounded almost as disappointed as a kid at not seeing any evidence of it.

"Be patient. It's not ready yet. When's Slade coming by?"

"Any minute now."

As if on cue, Josh shouted, "I think I hear the truck." He darted out the door, followed by Jamie at a more sedate, determinedly unconcerned pace.

Michael stepped closer to Grace and before she guessed his intentions, he bent down to give her a quick kiss. "Just so you know I'm glad to see you," he explained.

"You're just relieved those directions of yours panned out," she said.

"That, too," he said with a wink as he went outside to join the boys.

Grace laughed, suddenly feeling lighthearted. Then she turned to the serious task of baking a birthday cake for Josh. When she did it, baking ranked right up there with driving in its potential for disaster. But she'd put so much T.L.C. into this cake, it was bound to be a winner.

## Chapter Seven

Michael couldn't imagine what Grace had been up to, but the light shining in her eyes was long overdue. She looked happy, though he couldn't help wondering how much longer that would last.

He stood at the rail of the corral, one booted foot propped on the bottom rung and watched as Slade gave Josh and Jamie their lesson. Slade wasn't exactly talkative, but he knew horses. Both boys hung on every word the man said. They eagerly followed every instruction, right down to cleaning the tack and rubbing down the horses after their lesson. It seemed they were learning about responsibility right along with riding, soaking up not only the information, but the masculine attention. It reminded Michael just how badly they needed a male role model in their lives.

"Same time tomorrow?" Slade asked, joining him as the boys walked the horses.

"If you have the time," Michael said. "You can't begin to know what this means to those two."

"I think maybe I do," Slade said. "I get the sense they haven't had a lot."

"No."

"How'd they wind up here, if you don't mind me asking?"

"Long story," Michael said.

"Runaways," Slade guessed. He slanted a look at Michael. "I'm surprised you haven't turned 'em in. A lot of folks wouldn't have considered them their responsibility."

"Here in Los Piños?" Michael said skeptically. "I was under the impression that Harlan Adams set a tough example when it comes to being your brother's keeper around these parts."

"He does, now that you mention it. If he knew about Jamie and Josh, he'd see to it that something was done to help them, no doubt about it. You didn't tell him the whole story when you called over there looking for a riding instructor, did you?"

"No. I thought it best to be circumspect till we had more facts."

"Do you have them now?"

"Not really. Grace is still looking into some things."

"You need any help, White Pines is crawling with good-hearted people who love to meddle. Wouldn't hurt to have Justin Adams on your side. He's the sheriff. And, like I said, Harlan is a man you can always count on to sort out something that's gotten complicated. His wife knows the ins and outs of the law as well as anyone I've ever seen.''

"Thanks. I'll keep that in mind.''

Slade slanted a look his way. "I could bring my daughter Annie along tomorrow, if you like. She's a little older than Josh. I think they'd get along okay. And she knows all the other kids around here. She'd be happy to take these two under her wing and introduce them around. She knows what it's like to be an outsider. She had a rough patch when she first came to live with me, but she's adapted real well now.''

Michael shook his head at that. "Until Grace and I come up with a plan, the fewer people who know about Josh and Jamie the better. Bring Annie, by all means, but let's keep it at that for the time being.''

Slade nodded. "See you tomorrow, then.'' He touched a finger to his Stetson, then left for one last word with Jamie and Josh before taking off.

"What were you and Mr. Sutton talking about?'' Jamie asked when they finally returned from the barn after putting out feed for the horses.

"How well you're doing,'' Michael told him.

"He really said we were doing good?'' Josh asked excitedly. "Did you know he was a rodeo champion before his leg got busted up? If he says we're good, that's, like, the best.''

"Well, that's what he said. And I've noticed how responsible you're being about taking care of the horses. I'm proud of you both.''

"A cowboy's supposed to treat his horse right,'' Jamie retorted.

He said it as if it were a simple matter of doing

what was expected, as if their behavior were nothing special. But despite his words, it seemed to Michael that he stood a little taller because of the praise. He had to wonder how often anyone had bothered to tell the boy what he was doing right, rather than all the things he was doing wrong.

"Can we go inside and tell Grace about the lesson?" Josh pleaded.

Michael nodded, amazed to discover that he was almost as anxious as the boys to share the excitement with Grace. Once he had wanted to share everything with her, but long conversations about anything and everything had soon fallen by the wayside, lost to the demands of his position at Delacourt Oil and her studies in law school across the state.

"Let's go," he said. "But you'd better let me peek in the door first so we make sure we're not spoiling the big surprise."

"Yeah, that's right," Josh said. "She promised us something real special."

"Don't go getting all worked up," Jamie cautioned him. "It's probably just pot roast or something."

"But I love pot roast," Josh said.

"Yeah, but it's not a real surprise," Jamie countered. "It's just dinner."

Michael stayed out of the squabble, but he had a hunch the surprise was more than a good meal. Grace had been too excited.

"Stay right here on the back deck," Michael instructed the two of them. "I'll let you know if it's okay to come inside."

As soon as he was certain they would stay put, he

slipped into the house. He was struck at once by the aromas drifting from the direction of the kitchen, most of them enticing, though he thought he also detected something that might have been burnt sugar. Given that and the muttered cursing, he approached cautiously.

"Everything okay in here?" he inquired, drawing a startled look from the woman bent over in front of the oven. Her cheeks were streaked with flour and flushed from the heat, wisps of hair had curled against her forehead and her eyes flashed with indignation at whatever it was she'd been staring at in the oven. He thought she had never looked more beautiful.

"Everything except this blasted cake," she retorted. "It's lopsided." She withdrew the pan to show him. "Would you tell me why a woman who has mastered any number of skills cannot bake a simple chocolate cake?"

To be sure one side of the cake sank to no more than a half-inch, while the other side rose to a full, plump two inches.

"Is this cake going to be one layer or two?" he asked.

"Two, why?"

"Because you can fill in that crater with icing and no one will be the wiser. In fact, knowing how kids like icing, it'll probably be a huge hit."

Her expression immediately brightened. "You're a genius," she declared, giving him a smacking kiss on her way past. "Where are the boys?"

Michael barely resisted the desire to snag her by the apron strings and draw her back for a more leisurely exploration of her mouth. Instead, he said, "They're on the deck, chomping at the bit to get in here to see the surprise."

"Oh, dear, not yet," she protested at once. "I want everything to be perfect." She frowned at the cake. "Well, close to perfect, anyway. Send them upstairs for showers, but don't let them near the dining room."

"Yes, ma'am," Michael agreed. "On one condition?"

"What's that?" she asked, eyeing him warily.

"That I get to steal a kiss from the cook."

"I just kissed you," she pointed out.

He grinned. "Which makes it my turn. Do we have a deal?"

"Michael..."

The protest died as his mouth covered hers. She tasted of sugar and chocolate and smelled of roses. After a fleeting instant of resistance she melted against him, her body fitting itself to his as instinctively as it once had. Breasts, thighs, heat—they were all as familiar to him as the sigh of her breath against his cheek. He held her loosely, but she didn't even try to get away.

"I never said yes," she whispered.

"That's why they call it stealing," he reminded her. "Something tells me I could get into the habit of doing this again."

"Stealing?" she teased. "I suppose in this instance, I'd have to come to your defense. You're very good at it, Michael."

"I'll get better with practice."

She murmured something at that.

"What?"

"I said if you get any better, we'll have more trouble around here than having two runaways on our hands."

He regarded her with delight. "Sounds promising."

"Just go get the boys," she said. "I have work to do. I need an hour, okay?"

"Do you also need help?"

She regarded him with surprise. "From you?"

"Who else?"

"Since when do you help in the kitchen doing women's work?" she inquired tartly.

He winced at the too-accurate description of the way he'd been a few years ago, leaving everything connected to running their household to her. Fending for himself in recent years had changed all that. If he didn't cook these days, he didn't eat. Not at home, anyway.

"You'd be surprised at the things I've learned to do since you dumped me."

The claim seemed to fascinate her. "Then by all means join me back here and demonstrate," she said.

"Some of them will have to wait till we're alone in the house," he taunted, thoroughly enjoying the quick rise of color in her cheeks.

"I'll..." Her voice trailed off before she could complete the thought.

"You'll what?" he asked. "Look forward to it? Is that what you were about to say, Grace?"

"No, absolutely not," she denied unconvincingly. "I was about to say I'll be frosting this cake. The first batch of caramel sort of burned in the pan, but I think the second batch looks pretty good.''

He peered at the gooey, golden concoction. "If you say so."

"I do."

He gave her one last, skeptical look, then went off to shoo Jamie and Josh upstairs.

"Why can't we see what's going on?" Josh asked.

"Because Grace said so," Jamie told him. "It's a surprise, remember?"

"You're the one who said it probably wasn't a real surprise," Josh countered.

"Doesn't matter if it is or it isn't, we gotta do what Grace says. Now hurry up, and don't use all the hot water, either."

"It's not me," Josh protested. "You're the one who uses it all up."

Michael stood at the foot of the stairs listening to the bickering until it finally faded away. Once he'd expected to have sons of his own, expected to fill a house with laughter and sibling controversy, just like this. How had he lost sight of that part of his dream? Had it gone with the departure of Grace from his life, or even before, when he'd buried himself in work at Delacourt Oil just to prove himself?

Did it really matter when or how it had slipped away? he asked himself. Maybe what really mattered was whether it was too late to get it back....

## Chapter Eight

Grace took one last look around the dining room and gave a satisfied sigh. Balloons floated everywhere. The table had been set with Trish's best china and the gaily wrapped presents had been piled high at Josh's place.

"It looks terrific, darlin'," Michael said, coming up behind her to rest his hands on her shoulders. "Every little boy's dream birthday party."

"Do you think he'll mind that it's late?"

"No, something tells me that Josh will be over the moon that you thought to do it for him."

"I wonder how many birthday parties he's ever really had," Grace said, feeling sad for him. Her mom had always struggled to make birthdays special, even when they hadn't had much money to spend or when she hadn't had energy for anything else.

"My guess is not a lot," Michael replied. "Not if that was when Jamie always came for him."

"Will all this fuss over Josh bother Jamie?" she asked worriedly. "We don't even know when his birthday is."

"We'll find out and do something special for him, too," Michael reassured her.

"What if it's months from now?"

"We'll do it whenever it is," Michael insisted. "Wherever he is."

Grace sighed. "I hate to think of him being anywhere but here."

"I know. So do I. But let's be realistic. This isn't even our home. No matter what happens, he won't be here. Neither will we."

"But he's been so happy here the last couple of days. They both have."

"Then we'll look into finding them a home close by," Michael said.

He spoke so confidently as if it were as simple as choosing a place and having the kids move in. Maybe the matter-of-fact tone came from controlling a business empire. He was probably too used to people falling in with his plans. This time it might not be that simple, Grace thought.

"How?" Grace asked. "It's not like placing a puppy."

When he realized she wasn't going to be pacified by glib answers, he paused, his expression thoughtful. "Maybe Dylan's wife can help," he said eventually. "She's a pediatrician. She may know people who would be willing to take in a couple of boys.

Let's not talk about this tonight, though. Let's just have a party. I'll go call the boys, okay?''

Grace took one last survey, then nodded. "Go get them."

She waited with her heart in her throat until the two boys thundered down the stairs, then skidded to a stop in the entrance to the dining room.

"Oh, wow," Josh whispered, his gaze locked on the stack of presents. "Is this for me?"

Grace nodded. "I know it's a few days late, but I wanted you to have a celebration," she said.

"This is so cool." Josh raced across the room and threw his arms around her, all but knocking the breath out of her.

"I wish you were my mom," he whispered tearfully.

Grace felt her heart crack in two. "I wish I were, too," she whispered, her gaze seeking Michael's. "I wish I were, too."

She blinked back tears, then glanced toward Jamie, who was standing perfectly still, his expression shuttered.

"Jamie?"

He met her gaze. "What?"

"When is your birthday? Michael and I have already been talking about what we'll do then."

The disbelief in Jamie's eyes shifted slowly to hope. "You guys really talked about that?"

"Yes."

He shrugged. "We probably won't be around then. It's not till fall. September fifth. Sometimes I end up having to go back to school on my birthday. That really sucks."

Grace gave him a commiserating look. "I know. My birthday is September seventh."

"Looks like we'll be having a joint celebration this fall," Michael said, meeting Jamie's gaze evenly. "Sound okay to you?"

"Sure. I guess," Jamie said, clearly struggling still not to get his hopes up.

Michael nodded. "That's good then. Now how about sitting down before all this food gets cold?"

"When do I get to open my presents?" Josh asked.

"After we eat," Michael said firmly.

Grace shook her head. "No way. You can open them whenever you want to. It's your party."

Josh looked from her to Michael and back again, clearly wanting to please both of them. "I say I open one now and the rest after we eat."

"Good compromise," Michael praised. "You'll be a terrific businessman some day."

"Like you?" Josh asked.

"Probably better than him," Grace teased. "Michael's lousy at compromise."

"But I'm learning," he declared, winking at her. "I just need the proper incentive."

Clearly impatient, Josh interrupted them. "Can I open one now? Any one I want?"

"Yep," Grace said, then leaned closer. "But if I were you I'd pick that one." She pointed to the biggest box.

Josh grabbed it eagerly and began stripping away the paper. He tugged open the top without even glancing at the markings on the box, then stared, openmouthed, when he saw what was inside.

"What is it?" Jamie demanded. "You look like it's a snake or something."

"It's boots," Josh said, sounding awestruck. "Real cowboy boots."

"No way." Jamie stood up to peer over his shoulder. "I'll bet they're going to be too big."

"Are not," Josh said, taking one out of the box and holding it up next to his sneaker-clad foot.

Grace saw then that she had guessed wrong. The boot was definitely too big, but Josh was clearly undaunted. He kicked off his shoes and pulled the boots on.

"They're perfect," he declared. "See?" He clomped around the room.

"I think Jamie might be right," Michael said. "A cowboy doesn't want a boot that's not a perfect fit."

"But I love these," Josh said, near tears.

"We'll exchange them first thing tomorrow," Grace said, then glanced at Jamie who was eyeing the boots with longing. "I don't suppose these would fit you, would they, Jamie?"

Josh looked horrified. "He can't have my boots."

"If we're taking them back anyway, what difference does it make?" Grace asked reasonably. "You'll get new ones that are the perfect size for you tomorrow."

"Promise?" Josh asked.

"Of course, but you have to let him try them on so we know whether to trade these back in or just get you your own pair," Grace said.

"Can't I wear them for a little while?" Josh pleaded.

"No," Grace said firmly. "If we have to take them back, they can't be worn out."

Looking crestfallen, Josh sat back down and tugged off the boots, tossing them angrily at his big brother. Jamie threw them right back. "I don't want your old boots."

Grace saw the entire celebration falling apart. "That's enough," she said sternly. "No more presents till after we've eaten and if you two don't apologize to each other right now, there won't be any then either."

"It's just that I never had something that wasn't a hand-me-down before," Josh said to her.

Grace fought the sting of tears to remain firm. "That still doesn't mean you get to take out your disappointment on your brother. It's not his fault the boots might fit him instead of you. I'm the one who picked them out and bought the wrong size. Are you going to yell at me?"

Josh looked shocked by the suggestion. "Never."

"Okay, then, how about telling Jamie you're sorry?"

"I'm sorry," he said at once. "I hope they fit you."

Jamie shrugged. "I'm sorry, too."

Grace beamed at them. "That's better."

"Now can we eat?" Michael pleaded, breaking the tension. "I don't know about you guys, but I'm starving."

Grace sat back and watched as all three of them fell on the meal as if it were the best one they'd ever tasted. Heartfelt praise was uttered between mouthfuls.

"You guys are making me blush," she said eventually, but she couldn't help being pleased that the dinner was a bigger hit than the ill-fitting boots.

As soon as they'd eaten every last bite of pot roast, warm rolls and savory vegetables, she stood up and cleared the table. Jamie and Josh jumped up without being asked to help her take the dishes into the kitchen. Even Michael pitched in to get everything rinsed and into the dishwasher.

"Okay, everybody back to their places," she instructed. "I'll bring in the dessert."

Once they were gone, she stood for a moment alone, eyes closed as she savored the sensations that had washed through her over the last hour. She had felt as if she were finally, at long last, part of a real family. It didn't seem to matter that it was an illusion that could be shattered at any time. For now, all that counted was the fact that she was with a man she had once loved more than life itself and with two little boys who desperately needed a mother and father to love them. She would do anything necessary to spin out this perfect time for as long as possible...for all their sakes.

The cake, with its eight flickering candles and thick caramel frosting, was a huge hit. So were the rest of the presents Grace had brought back from town.

While Grace watched Josh's reaction, Michael kept his gaze focused on her. There was so much love shining in her eyes that it worried him. As if he could read her mind, he knew that she was starting to make plans for these two boys, thinking ahead to a future that was more than likely built on quicksand. She needed a harsh reality check, but he didn't want to be the one to give it to her. How could he, when he was the one who'd dragged her into this? And yet he knew he had no choice.

Later, when she had tucked the boys into bed—not even Jamie had protested that tonight—Michael was waiting for her in the living room with every light blazing. He'd resisted the temptation to spend the rest of the evening on the deck, under the stars. There were too many possible distractions in such a romantic setting. His body was sending too many demanding messages every time he and Grace were alone.

Here, with bright lights to chase away the shadows, they could engage in some straight talk, make realistic, practical plans. In this lighting, maybe he wouldn't get lost in the fantasy himself.

He spent the time while she was gone ticking off all of the rational reasons for putting an end to this situation here and now, not the least of which was the legal tightrope they were walking.

But when Grace walked into the room, looking sad and vulnerable—desirable—every rational thought in his head fled. He realized with stunned amazement that he wanted her, not just for tonight, but for all time. He knew with absolute certainty that he couldn't let her get away again, that if he did he would regret it for the rest of his days.

Unfortunately, he also knew she wasn't ready to hear such a declaration. She wouldn't trust it any more now than she had six years ago. Actions, not words, were the only way to convince her that he was ready to bring some balance in his life. Wouldn't Tyler find it a hoot that in sending his big brother here to get away from it all, to gain a little perspective in his life, he had actually accomplished his goal in a thoroughly unexpected way?

Of course, there was one little problem. He could hardly start out proving his love to Grace by telling her that she had to turn her back on those two boys. Once those words were out of his mouth, she was going to hate him.

He felt her gaze settle on him, saw worry pucker her brow.

"Michael, is something wrong?"

"Of course not," he lied. "Why?"

"You look so sad. I don't think I've ever seen you look like that before."

"Not sad, just concerned," he said, broaching the unavoidable topic of Jamie and Josh cautiously, hoping to minimize the damage to their future.

"About?"

"Your attachment to Jamie and Josh."

"I just threw a little party," she insisted staunchly. "What's the big deal?"

"We both know the answer to that," he chided. "Grace, my bringing you here was a mistake. You're a professional. It never occurred to me that you would get this emotionally involved. It should have, but it didn't."

She regarded him with obvious impatience. "We've been all through that. I'm here now. I'm right in the thick of this."

"But at what cost?"

"Dammit, Michael, I'm a big girl. You worry about your heart and I'll worry about mine."

He regarded her with regret. "If only it were that easy."

"It's as easy as you let it be."

"No, Grace, it's not. I've already been responsible for one heartbreak in your life. I won't be responsible for another." He drew in a deep breath. "We can't put it off any longer. We have to deal with this tomorrow."

She stared at him with what could only be interpreted as panic in her eyes. "Deal with it how?"

"Call the authorities. Let them know Jamie and Josh are safe."

She was on her feet at once. "No. They'll take them away," she said, voicing what was clearly her greatest fear.

"They might," he agreed.

"I won't let you do it, Michael." Tears streaked down her cheeks. "I can't. It's wrong. You know it's wrong."

"I don't know that. Neither do you. If anything, you know the law better than I do. You have to see that we can't postpone this. We're heading for disaster as it is."

For a moment she looked as if she might argue some more, but then a shudder shook her body, even as the tears continued to track silently down her cheeks. He'd seen her like this only one other time, the day she had told him that she didn't want to see him ever again. Since then, she had never let him see any sign of weakness. If anything, she was tough as nails whenever she had to confront him.

He swore under his breath, cursing himself for calling her in the first place, for not finding some other way to deal with the two runaways now sleeping upstairs.

"Dammit, Grace, don't do this," he pleaded.

"Do what?" she asked without meeting his gaze.

"Make me feel like a jerk."

"As if I could," she shot back, showing a little more spirit.

But even then the tears didn't let up. Michael went to her then and pulled her into his arms, let her tears soak his shirt. She didn't resist. In fact, she probably took perverse pleasure in ruining the pristine condition of his silk-blend shirt. She could ruin a hundred of them, as far as he was concerned, if only she would forgive him for what he was insisting they do.

Oh, he knew that in the end she would come around, do what had to be done, because she was too wise not to see that it was the only way. In the meantime, though, he could hold her close, maybe let her see by his actions that even after Jamie and Josh were gone, he would still be here for her.

Sadly, though, he suspected that after this, she might not consider him a fit substitute, might not want him at all.

Grace was too numb after Michael's announcement to even try to break away from his attempt to console her. Eventually, though, she retreated upstairs, angrily tugged on her nightgown, tried to settle in bed, then gave up in frustration as she thought of all the arguments she should have flung at him.

What was wrong with her? She didn't fall apart in

a crisis. She got tougher, especially if Michael Delacourt was involved. She had vowed six years ago that he would never see her cry again. Now here she was blubbering, instead of doing what she did best, instead of fighting tooth and nail for what she believed.

And what she believed with all her heart was that Jamie and Josh deserved a better shot than they'd been given. Instead of coming unglued, she should have been making calls, rallying allies who could make that happen for them.

She paced her room for a while, debating alternatives to Michael's plan to call in the authorities, but nothing she came up with made a lick of sense. In the end, bottom line, the authorities would have to be notified. Did it really matter if it was tomorrow or the next day? Once they were on the scene, the real work of fighting for Josh and Jamie would begin. Maybe it was better if it began sooner, rather than later. She always focused better once the fight had begun.

That acceptance of the inevitable didn't mean she wasn't sorely tempted to steal down the hall, wake the boys and spirit them away from the house while Michael was sleeping. Only the knowledge that he would probably catch them in the act kept her from trying it.

She was determined about one thing, though. No call would be made until after she and Michael had made good on their promise to take Josh into town for new boots. There were no guarantees for the future, but she refused to renege on that particular promise. Something told her there would be enough broken promises to come after that.

Bracing herself to fight Michael over her decision, if need be, she was in the kitchen at dawn making waffles. When the boys came downstairs, they were subdued, as if they sensed that something had happened.

"You okay?" Jamie asked, studying her. "You look kinda funny, like you been crying or something."

"I'm fine," Grace reassured him.

Jamie didn't look convinced. "If Michael's made you cry, Josh and me will beat him up for you," he said gamely.

Grace bit back a smile. "I don't think that will be necessary."

"Are you guys, like, dating or something?" Josh asked.

"We did a long time ago," Grace said. "Now we're just friends." Even as she said it, she realized it was true. Despite all the pain, Michael was her friend. His decision had been made the night before not to be cruel to Jamie and Josh, but, as he saw it, to protect her.

"Oh," Josh said, clearly disappointed.

He and Jamie exchanged a look she couldn't interpret.

"Me and Josh have been talking. We were kinda hoping it was more than that," Jamie explained.

"Oh? Why?" Grace asked, though she thought she knew.

"'Cause if you were gonna get married, then maybe you could be our new foster parents," Jamie said, then sighed. "I guess that won't work, though, will it?"

Now there was a solution she hadn't considered. She could just imagine Michael's reaction to such a suggestion. Once he stopped laughing, the answer would be a resounding no. He didn't have time to fit a wife into his life, much less two boys.

"No," Grace said. "I'm sorry."

"Couldn't you be our foster mom, though?" Josh asked hopefully.

The very same idea had occurred to her more than once in the past forty-eight hours, but Grace had dismissed it as illogical and impractical. A pipe dream.

But was it? She was as qualified as anyone. She had the financial resources. She already cared deeply for the two of them.

She sighed. She also had a one-bedroom apartment and a demanding law career. How could she possibly bring two young boys into her life and give them the time and attention they needed? And it wasn't as if she could walk into the courthouse, make the offer and walk out with them. There were background checks and mounds of paperwork involved.

As her mental debate raged on, the boys watched her intently, clearly sensing that she was actually struggling with their suggestion.

"So, what do you think?" Jamie finally dared to ask.

"I don't know," she said honestly. "This is a very complicated situation." Probably more so, precisely because she had kept them here, rather than turning them in immediately. The court would probably view that as blatant evidence that she had no regard at all for the regulations governing foster care.

"We'd be really good," Josh promised.

"Yeah, we wouldn't give you any problems. No more running away or nothing," Jamie vowed. "And we can help around the house and stuff, do a lot of chores like taking out the trash."

"I'm sure you'd be a wonderful help, but I just don't know. There are a lot of things to consider before making a commitment like that."

"It's because there are two of us, isn't it?" Jamie said, sounding defeated. "If that's it, take Josh. I'll go someplace else."

"Absolutely not," Grace said at once. "You're not going to be separated again. I'm going to see to that, no matter what." She game Jamie's shoulder a squeeze. "Let me give this some more thought, okay? I'm not ruling it out, but I'm not saying yes either."

"Think really, really hard," Josh pleaded. "We need you, Grace."

Jamie's gaze locked on hers, regarding her with an understanding that was wise beyond his years. Then he turned to Josh. "Stop bugging her, okay? Let her think."

"Think about what?" Michael asked, walking into the kitchen in jeans and a dress shirt with the sleeves rolled up and the collar open. His hair was still damp from a shower.

Grace's heart skipped a beat as the vivid memory of several steamy, shared showers rushed back. It had been six years and she hadn't been able to shake the way the man made her feel with just a glance. She could all but feel his hands on her body, feel him deep inside her. The memory alone was enough to make her cheeks burn.

Right now, though, he was a threat to this make-believe family of hers. He wanted to tear the four of them apart with what he viewed as a necessary phone call. And even though she knew in her head that he was right, in her heart she suspected she might wind up hating him for it.

"Okay, everybody, eat up," she said as she placed plates of waffles and bacon on the table. "As soon as we've finished breakfast, we're going into town."

She regarded Michael with a touch of defiance as she said it, daring him to contradict her announcement.

"We'll get Josh's new boots, maybe do a little shopping, then have lunch," she added for good measure. "I vote for pizza. How about the rest of you?"

"All right!" Josh enthused.

"Pizza's okay by me, too," Jamie responded.

Grace met Michael's gaze. "And you? Any objections?"

"Not a one," he said, regarding her with a look that spoke volumes.

It was evident he intended to keep silent about any real objections until they were alone. Grace just had to make sure that didn't happen. She didn't need another well-intentioned lecture. She had a few more hours at most with Jamie and Josh. She wasn't going to have them spoiled by nagging reminders that time was running out.

She actually managed to avoid being alone with

Michael until after they got into Los Piños. As Jamie and Josh raced ahead to the shop where she had bought the cowboy boots, Michael clasped her arm in a firm grip and held her back.

"This is a temporary reprieve, because you made him a promise, understood?"

She frowned at his commanding tone. "This is not your decision to make," she retorted.

"Maybe not entirely," he agreed. "But I've made it, because I don't think you can."

"And the rest of us just have to live with it, is that it? This isn't Delacourt Oil, Michael. You're not the boss. We're equal partners," she declared, then added pointedly, "All four of us."

He regarded her with evident frustration. "You can't expect Jamie and Josh to know what's in their best interests."

"And you do?" she retorted. "Mr. No-time-for-anything-that-isn't-business? Who made you an expert in child-rearing? My hunch is you don't even spend any time with your niece and nephews, except maybe holidays."

His pained expression told her she'd gotten it exactly right.

"Okay, Grace, maybe I'm not a dad, maybe I'm not even the most involved uncle in the world, but I can spot a disaster when it's just waiting to happen. We've got to settle this today. Those boys are getting too attached to you and you to them. It's not good."

She knew he was right and, as she'd anticipated, she despised him for it. "Fine. You make that call whenever you decide it's right. I'm going to get those boots for Josh."

She jerked out of his grasp and stalked down the block. Of course, he caught up with her before she reached the store.

"Sweetheart, I'm not the bad guy here."

"Couldn't prove it by me," she said.

"Do you think I want those boys to go back to the kind of lives they were living? Do you think I can't see how awful it was for them to be separated? Hell, I think about something like that happening to me, Tyler, Dylan and Jeb and I can't even imagine it."

"Then help me to do something," she pleaded, gazing up at him. "Don't make that call until we have a real plan, one that nobody with any sense of decency can challenge."

Michael raked a hand through his hair, his expression torn. "Grace—"

Sensing that he was weakening, she made one more plea. "Please. I've never begged for anything from you before, Michael, but I'm begging now. Not for myself, for Jamie and Josh. They deserve a real chance, a real family."

He visibly struggled with her request. "We'll make that plan this afternoon, though, right? No more putting it off?"

"I swear it," she said. "The four of us will sit down and think of something as soon as we get back to the ranch."

"No," he corrected. "You and I will make the decision. Then we'll sell it to the boys together. Deal?"

She had a feeling it was the best she was going to get. "Deal," she agreed.

She started to move away, but Michael snagged her hand again. "Grace?"

She lifted her gaze to his.

"I love it that you care so much."

She sighed. She couldn't help wondering what he'd say if he knew that over the last two days she'd realized that she cared just as much about him.

## Chapter Nine

At the Italian restaurant, Josh could barely sit still. He kept poking his feet out to stare at his new boots. Then he'd get up and clomp around the table, trying to imitate the rolling gait of a cowboy. Apparently he'd watched a lot of westerns, since as far as Michael knew he'd never met any real cowboy besides Slade and Slade walked with a limp thanks to a tragic accident that had cost him his rodeo career and almost his life.

"I think he likes the boots," Grace noted.

"What was your first clue?" Michael responded, chuckling.

"He's acting like a jerk," Jamie declared with adolescent disdain. "They're just shoes."

Michael exchanged an amused look with Grace, then regarded Jamie intently. "Guess that means you'd rather we'd gotten you something else, instead of letting you keep the boots that were too big for Josh.''

Jamie squirmed uncomfortably. "Nah, they're cool."

"Then let's not make fun of your brother," Michael chided.

"Yeah, whatever."

Grace grinned at Jamie. "There's one advantage to Josh being away from the table," she leaned over to confide.

"What?"

"More pizza for you."

Jamie's expression brightened. "Hey, yeah. Gimme that last piece." He was already reaching for it, when he thought better of it. He glanced at Michael. "You want it?"

"No, but you might check with Grace."

"It was her idea for me to take it."

"Ask anyway. It's only polite."

Jamie rolled his eyes, but he dutifully turned to Grace. "You want another piece of pizza?"

"No, it's all yours."

Jamie shot a triumphant look at Michael. "Told you so," he said, grabbing the piece and taking a huge bite out of it to stake his claim.

As soon as he'd wolfed down the pizza, he went off to join Josh, who was watching some kids play the video games at the back of the restaurant. In minutes, he was back again.

"Could we have some quarters to play?" he asked. "We'll do extra work at the ranch to earn them."

## The Silhouette Reader Service™ — Here's how it works:

Accepting your 2 free books and gift places you under no obligation to buy anything. You may keep the books and gift and return the shipping statement marked "cancel." If you do not cancel, about a month later we'll send you 6 additional novels and bill you just $3.80 each in the U.S., or $4.21 each in Canada, plus 25¢ shipping & handling per book and applicable taxes if any.* That's the complete price and — compared to cover prices of $4.50 each in the U.S. and $5.25 each in Canada — it's quite a bargain! You may cancel at any time, but if you choose to continue, every month we'll send you 6 more books, which you may either purchase at the discount price or return to us and cancel your subscription.

*Terms and prices subject to change without notice. Sales tax applicable in N.Y. Canadian residents will be charged applicable provincial taxes and GST.

NO POSTAGE
NECESSARY
IF MAILED
IN THE
UNITED STATES

If offer card is missing write to: Silhouette Reader Service, 3010 Walden Ave., P.O. Box 1867, Buffalo NY 14240-1867

## BUSINESS REPLY MAIL
FIRST-CLASS MAIL    PERMIT NO. 717    BUFFALO, NY

POSTAGE WILL BE PAID BY ADDRESSEE

SILHOUETTE READER SERVICE
3010 WALDEN AVE
PO BOX 1867
BUFFALO NY 14240-9952

# Play The Lucky Hearts Game

### and get...

## FREE BOOKS & a FREE GIFT...
## YOURS to KEEP!

**Yes!** I have scratched off the silver card. Please send me my **2 FREE BOOKS** and **FREE MYSTERY GIFT**. I understand that I am under no obligation to purchase any books as explained on the back of this card.

**Scratch Here!**
then look below to see what your cards get you...

335 SDL C6KF                                    235 SDL C6KA

| | | | | | | | | | | | | | | | |

NAME                          (PLEASE PRINT CLEARLY)

| | | | | | | | | | | | | | | | |

ADDRESS

| | | | | | | | | | | | | | | | |

APT.#                         CITY

| | | | | | | | | | | | | | | | |

STATE/PROV.                                   ZIP/POSTAL CODE

DETACH AND MAIL CARD TODAY! (S-SE-OS-10/00)

Twenty-one gets you
**2 FREE BOOKS** and a
**FREE MYSTERY GIFT!**

Twenty gets you
**2 FREE BOOKS!**

Nineteen gets you
**1 FREE BOOK!**

**TRY AGAIN!**

Offer limited to one per household and not valid to current Silhouette Special Edition® subscribers. All orders subject to approval.

Visit us online at
www.eHarlequin.com

Michael was impressed with Jamie's willingness to work for the money. The kid had learned a lot of lessons, either from the foster parents he claimed to disdain or from his struggles to make it on his own whenever he came for Josh. He took nothing for granted. He expected to work for whatever he got.

Michael handed him a couple of dollars. "Ask them to change them for you at the register," he said. "Consider it payment for the work you've already done feeding the horses."

"Thanks," Jamie said.

"Those kids are so eager to please," Michael said. "How could they have given their foster parents so much trouble?"

"Maybe we're seeing another side of them just because they're so grateful to be together," Grace suggested.

"You ever see a kid who could pull off a charade like this for more than a few minutes at a time? These are good kids, Grace."

"I'm not about to argue with you. I think they're terrific. But maybe we're seeing them at their best, because they see us as their last chance," Grace said quietly.

Michael didn't know what to say to that. But he did know a lot about last chances. If this was the last one he was going to have with Grace, then he was going to have to make the most of it. He glanced at her, saw the wistful way she was staring at Jamie and Josh.

What was she hoping for, really? Did she merely want to find them a home where they could be together? Would she be satisfied with that? Or was she imagining providing a home for them herself?

He thought about the latter and had the oddest feeling that his own expression was probably every bit as wistful as hers. Was he beginning to want the same thing? Not just Grace, Jamie and Josh as a family, but with himself in the picture, too? He wanted Grace back in his life, but did he want the rest? Marriage? A family? Was he truly ready to make the necessary changes in his lifestyle?

The pitiful truth was that his work habits were as ingrained as breathing. His days were crowded from morning to night. Was that because he liked it that way, because it had to be that way? Or because he didn't have anything else he cared about as deeply?

And how the hell was he supposed to figure out the answer in the next couple of hours? Suddenly he regretted setting a deadline, but he knew he couldn't back off now. That deadline was as right now as it had been when he'd insisted on it.

That didn't mean he couldn't nudge it back just a little.

"Hey, Josh, Jamie," he called, drawing a worried look from Grace. "How about going down to Dolan's for ice cream?"

"Hot fudge sundaes?" Josh asked eagerly.

"You bet," Michael agreed. "Grace? Is that okay with you?"

As if she understood that he was offering more than scoops of ice cream, her frown faded and a smile spread slowly across her face. "Have you ever known me to turn down a hot fudge sundae?"

"Now that you mention it, no. It was the one way

I always knew I could lure you away from your law books.''

''Not the only way,'' she teased with a surprising glint in her eyes.

Michael recalled the other way all too clearly. ''Maybe we'd better stick to the G-rated method for now, though I am definitely up for the alternative anytime you give the word.''

''Is that so?'' she asked with amusement.

''Oh, yes,'' he said fervently. ''Try me.''

''Maybe I will,'' she said thoughtfully.

Jamie and Josh scowled at them. ''Are you two coming or not?''

''We're coming,'' Grace said, sashaying past Michael with a provocative sway to her hips.

He shook his head as he enjoyed the view. The woman was definitely dangerous. In the last few minutes he had not only tossed aside his common sense where those kids were concerned, he was about to invite Grace Foster back into his bed, back into his life. He wasn't sure which of them would be in more trouble if she said yes.

Grace wondered how smart it had been to come to Dolan's when she saw Sharon Lynn's eyes light up with fascination the instant they walked in the door. She had a hunch they were about to be treated to a display of the famed Adams meddling.

''Well, well, well, who do we have here?'' she asked, her gaze traveling from Grace to Michael to the boys and back. She eventually settled on Michael. ''You must be Trish's brother. I can see the family resemblance, even though I barely caught a glimpse of you at Dylan's wedding.''

"Guilty," he agreed. "Michael Delacourt."

"And I'm Sharon Lynn Branson."

"She's an Adams," Grace inserted pointedly, just so Michael would know what they were dealing with. It was apparent from his expression that he got the message.

"I've heard about you," he told Sharon Lynn.

"Oh, I'll just bet you have," she said, laughing. "Stories about this family tend to get around."

"I was thinking of the way you helped Trish with her grand opening. She said it was wildly successful because of you and your family."

"We were just being neighborly," Sharon Lynn insisted, her gaze shifting to the boys. "Now, then, I know Michael and I've met Grace, but who are you two handsome boys?"

Again, Grace was quick to step in. "This is Josh and this is Jamie. They're visiting us."

"Oh, really?" she said. "Nice to meet you, Josh and Jamie."

Grace had the feeling from Sharon Lynn's vaguely curious expression that she wanted to say a lot more, but about that time a toddler crept into view from behind the counter. As if she were satisfied that her mother's attention was elsewhere, she took off toward a shelf full of first aid supplies. Before anyone could react, she had tumbled boxes of bandages on the floor and was trying to get into one of them.

Sharon Lynn sighed as she scooped her up, ignoring the wails of protest.

"Got a boo-boo," the baby insisted tearfully. She turned to Grace, apparently sensing a softhearted ally. "See?"

"Yes, indeed," Grace said, though she saw nothing of the kind. "A very bad boo-boo. Maybe a kiss from mommy would be better than a bandage, though."

Deep blue eyes, swimming in tears, brightened. "Kiss?" she repeated, peering at Sharon Lynn.

"You are such a little manipulator," Sharon Lynn declared, but she dutifully kissed the outstretched finger. "Is that better?"

The child nodded happily. "Boo-boo all gone."

"I'll pick up the boxes," Jamie said, already lining them up neatly on the shelves.

Sharon Lynn gaped. "Who raised him? There's not a kid in our entire clan who would volunteer that fast for any kind of cleanup."

"He's one of a kind, all right," Michael agreed.

Sharon Lynn thrust her daughter into his arms. "Take her for a sec, okay? I'll help Jamie get everything back, then I'll be right over to take your order."

"I'll help, too," Josh offered, already tagging along behind her.

"That's okay. I think Jamie and I can handle it." She flashed a grin at Josh. "Looks to me like Michael might need you more than I do."

Michael stood there, a shocked expression on his face, the toddler held away from his body like a painting he was inspecting closely before deciding whether to buy. She beamed at him.

"I think she likes you," Grace said.

"She's pretty cool," Josh decided after a thorough survey. "I ain't never been around anybody littler than me."

It was pretty clear that Michael hadn't been around many people that size either. Grace finally took pity on him and took the toddler. He shot her a relieved look and headed for a stool at the counter. She had a feeling if it had been a bar, he might have ordered a double.

Enjoying the feel of the little girl snuggled in her arms, Grace took a seat next to him. "Don't tell me you were scared by a little bitty thing like this," she teased.

"I was not scared," he protested.

But when the child started to scramble toward him, reaching out her arms, he looked as panicked as Grace had ever seen him. "You sure about that?" she asked.

He frowned. "Of course, I'm sure. It's not like I get a lot of opportunities to be around babies. I don't want to slip up, that's all."

"So, before you have kids of your own, you'll buy some books, study up?"

"Exactly."

Grace suddenly had a vision of Michael poring over baby books with the same intensity he devoted to geological surveys. Maybe that was how he would approach having a family of his own, all out. Maybe the trick was to convince him that it was something he wanted as badly as he had always wanted the presidency of Delacourt Oil.

And who was she to make fun of his inexperience? It wasn't as if she'd spent a lot of time around children. Once her relationship with Michael had ended, she had put any thoughts of family on a back burner herself. Her friends tended to be other fast-track lawyers who, even if married, had put off having children. Those who had them spent pitifully little time at home with them.

So why was she suddenly being swamped by all these maternal sentiments? Was it the situation with Josh and Jamie? Was it holding this squirming little angel in her arms? Or was it being back with Michael again, thinking about having a family specifically with him the way she'd once dreamed of?

She feared it was the latter, more than anything. After all those childhood insecurities about abandonment, he was the only man who'd ever made her yearn for happily ever after. He was the only one she'd been able to see herself sitting with on a front porch in fifty years, her mind every bit as engaged as her heart. She'd put all those longings on hold for six long years and now, thanks to a few days of close proximity, they were coming back in a flood.

Before she could wonder where all that was likely to lead, Sharon Lynn stepped back behind the counter.

"I understand we're looking at hot fudge sundaes all around."

"That's the plan," Michael agreed.

"With lots of whipped cream," Josh added.

"And nuts," Grace chimed in.

"My favorite kind of customers," Sharon Lynn said. "No cholesterol worries in this crowd."

"Not today, anyway," Grace agreed.

"Is this a celebration?" Sharon Lynn asked as she began scooping vanilla ice cream into old-fashioned glass dishes.

Grace glanced at Michael, saw the glimmer of uneasiness in his eyes. "Not exactly," she said. "Just a treat."

"Yeah," Josh enthused. "We've been getting lots of treats. I even got new cowboy boots. Jamie, too." He stuck out his feet so Sharon Lynn could see over the counter.

"Very handsome," she approved. "How are the riding lessons going?"

At Grace's startled look, she said, "The White Pines grapevine is an extraordinary thing. Not much goes on out there that I don't hear about. Slade's daughter Annie and his wife are two of my best customers. I love 'em. They talk a mile a minute. Even if they didn't, Grandpa Harlan would have filled me in."

Michael's gaze narrowed. "Harlan Adams? He knows about the boys and the lessons? I only told him about needing riding lessons. I thought he'd assume they were for me."

She nodded. "Grandpa Harlan has sources from one end of the state to the next. It's a waste of time trying to keep anything from him."

Michael's expression sobered. "I see."

Sharon Lynn regarded him worriedly. "Is that a problem?"

"I honestly don't know," Michael said.

Grace picked up on his anxiety and studied him warily. "Michael, what are you thinking?"

"That we shouldn't have gotten sidetracked from my original plan. Too many people already know."

"Know what?" Jamie asked with his usual unabashed curiosity.

"That you're staying out at Trish's with Grace and me," Michael said.

Jamie's expression fell, his mood suddenly as dark as Michael's. "That's a bad thing, isn't it?"

"Let's just say I wish the word hadn't spread quite so far."

Sharon Lynn caught what he said as she put the sundaes on the counter in front of them. "Look, I'm not sure what the deal is, but you don't have to worry about anybody in the family blabbing your business to outsiders. If it's possible for a grapevine to be discreet, ours is."

"I hope so," Michael said fervently. "Otherwise we could be looking at a whole heap of trouble."

The instant the uncensored remark was out of Michael's mouth, alarm spread across Jamie's face. He stuck his spoon back in his ice cream and pushed it away. Grace reached over and moved it back.

"There is no need for you to worry," she told him quietly. "Michael and I will handle anything that comes up." She gazed at Michael. "Right?"

"Absolutely," he said with more conviction than he probably felt.

"Promise?" Jamie asked.

"You have my word on it."

"But—"

"Jamie, I promise," she said solemnly.

Finally reassured, Jamie dug into his sundae, polishing it off in no time. Josh, who'd been too busy scraping every last bit of hot fudge out of the bottom of the dish to pay attention to the tension swirling around him, finished up and climbed off of the stool.

"Can Jamie and me go for a walk around town?" he asked.

"If you don't leave Main Street," Michael said.

Grace regarded him with surprise. "Are you sure—?"

"It'll be fine."

After they'd gone, she sighed. "Jamie's scared. Are you sure they won't just take off?"

"I'm as sure of that as I am of anything," Michael said. "Which isn't saying a lot right now."

Sharon Lynn came around and sat on the stool next to Grace, the baby settled in her lap with a dog-eared picture book. "Obviously I set off a panic earlier. Why don't you fill me in? Maybe I can help."

"Maybe we do need an objective opinion. You and I are a little too close to the situation," Grace said, trying to gauge Michael's reaction. He finally nodded.

With that go-ahead, Grace gave Sharon Lynn a brief summary of the situation.

"Those poor boys," Sharon Lynn murmured more than once.

"Any ideas about how we can keep them together?" Michael asked. "Grace and I are both committed to making that happen."

"How would you feel if I held a family pow-wow?" Sharon Lynn asked. "All of us have big homes. And nobody's more devoted to the concept of family than an Adams. Surely among us we could come up with a place for them to stay so they'd be together. Then we could go to social services, present them with a solution they couldn't possibly refuse.

I'm living proof that the tactic can work. What do you think?''

"Are you sure there are people in your family who would consider taking in two boys they haven't even met yet?'' Grace worried.

"I know it,'' Sharon Lynn said. "I'd have to talk to Cord, of course, but I'd do it in a heartbeat. I always wanted a ton of kids around. We don't have as much room as some of the others, but we could make it work.''

Grace thought of those dry legal pages that had summarized Sharon Lynn's battle for custody of the little girl who had been left on her doorstep. She saw that same kind of commitment and love shining in her eyes now. Jamie and Josh would definitely be in good hands with Sharon Lynn.

So, why did she feel so empty inside thinking of the boys staying right here with a woman like Sharon Lynn as their mother? Why was saying no her immediate reaction?

Because she wanted them for herself, she realized with a sinking sense of loss. She couldn't delude herself that her response was anything other than pure jealousy over the fact that Sharon Lynn had a family to offer them. It was a selfish, knee-jerk reaction.

"Well?'' Sharon Lynn asked. "What do you think?''

Michael's gaze settled on hers. "Grace?''

"It's an option,'' she said slowly, trying to hide her dismay. "You're very generous to even consider the idea.''

"Shall I talk to Cord and the others? See if we come up with any other brilliant solutions?''

"I think we should let her," Michael said. "Right, Grace?"

Grace forced herself to nod agreement, because she wasn't sure she could speak around the sudden lump in her throat.

"And in the meantime, I think maybe you should talk to my cousin Justin," Sharon Lynn went on. "If you've filled the local sheriff in, you might avoid any problems about letting the boys stay here, rather than turning them in the second you discovered them in the barn. Justin can take his own sweet time about filing paperwork when it suits him. Not that he approves of such things, but one look at those boys and how happy they are and I think in this instance it will suit him just fine."

"Thanks, Sharon Lynn," Michael said. "I think we'll do exactly that. Now we'd better go round up those two and get them back out to Trish's, before anybody else starts asking questions about who they are and where they came from."

Trying to make up for her earlier lack of enthusiasm, Grace gave Sharon Lynn a hug. "You really are wonderful. Your kids are very lucky."

"No," Sharon Lynn said fervently. "I'm the lucky one. I've got the sexiest, most loving husband on the planet and three great kids. Why not share that if I can? I'll call you all later and let you know how things turn out when I talk to the family."

Outside, Grace spotted Jamie and Josh peering in the window of the feed and grain store. They seemed perfectly content for the moment, so she turned to Michael.

"Do you think we should call Justin?"

"I think it might be the smart thing to do," he said. "If he's anything like Sharon Lynn, he'll be on our side. That can't hurt."

"What if he's not?" Grace asked worriedly. "What if he's a by-the-book kind of guy?"

"Dylan says he is," Michael admitted. "But he also says there's no one he'd rather have on his side in a fight."

"How well does Dylan really know him?"

"They worked together when Kelsey's son was missing. Dylan said the only thing that mattered to Justin was getting the boy back, not which rules might have been bent in the process. He even considered going to work for Justin as a deputy. For Dylan to even think about doing that, the man has to be a good guy."

He studied Grace. "You're not convinced, are you? Not about any of it, including Sharon Lynn's willingness to take the boys in if her husband agrees."

"How can I not be glad about that?" she said, but she couldn't manage to force any enthusiasm into her voice.

Michael touched a hand to her cheek. "Grace?"

She forced herself to meet his gaze, saw the concern in his expression. "What?"

"What's really going on here? No evasions this time. I want the truth."

"I don't know," she said honestly.

"You want those boys to stay with you, don't you?" he said, putting into words what she'd been afraid to say.

Her breath caught at the accuracy of his assessment. It had been a long time since anyone had been able to see into her heart like that, since anyone had even tried. She owed him an honest answer.

"I know it's not realistic, that it doesn't make any kind of sense, but yes, I want to keep them in my life," she admitted.

"In your life?" he asked skeptically. "You could do that no matter where they wind up. You really want them with you permanently. I can see it when you look at them. It's exactly what I was afraid of."

"I know it's wrong, even selfish," she finally conceded, then regarded him fiercely. "But, yes, that is exactly what I want. Those boys need a loving home and I want to be the one to give it to them."

"What about your career?"

"I can make it work," she insisted. "I wouldn't be the first woman to have to juggle work and parenting."

"But two kids, out of the blue?" he asked skeptically. "Jamie and Josh are trying really hard right now to do everything they can to please you, but it won't always be that way. Jamie's a teenager. Teenaged boys can be a handful. Are you prepared for that?"

"Yes," she said without hesitation. She might be good for Josh and Jamie, but they would bring even more into her life, something that had been missing for as long as she could remember.

Michael cupped her chin in his palm, his gaze locked with hers, as if he were searching for assurance that she had no doubts about her claim. Apparently satisfied with what he saw, he nodded. "Then we'll do what we can to make it happen."

Her heart leaped at the conviction she heard in his voice, the certainty that everything would be settled just the way she wanted it. Given Michael's reputation as a determined man and a tough negotiator, she didn't doubt for an instant that he could make it happen.

But then what? Despite her brave words, how would she manage if she won?

What had he gone and done, Michael worried as he sat up late that night while Grace and the boys slept upstairs. How was he supposed to keep his promise to her? And, for that matter, how did he feel about her determination to bring Jamie and Josh into her life on a full-time basis? Would there be room for him in that equation? Did he want there to be?

When he could no longer stand the way his thoughts kept shifting back and forth with no resolution in sight, he picked up the phone and called Tyler, waking him out of a sound sleep.

"Michael?" his brother asked sleepily. "What's going on? It's the middle of the night. Don't you have something better to do, or did Grace go home?"

"Grace is asleep," he said, then drew in a deep breath. "So are the two boys I discovered hiding out in the barn."

Tyler's sharp intake of breath suggested he'd finally come awake in a hurry.

"Michael, what the devil is going on over there?"

"You have no idea," Michael said wryly. "But I think I could use a friendly face."

"And you'd prefer mine to Grace's? You obviously need another lecture on your priorities."

"It's gotten complicated," Michael said. "Since you got me over here, I figure you owe me."

"I'll be there first thing in the morning," Tyler agreed at once. "It might be a real good time for me to be out of town anyway."

Something in his little brother's voice alerted Michael that he wasn't the only one with a lot on his mind. "Ty, is everything okay?"

"Nothing I can't handle with a little fancy footwork," Tyler assured him. "See you in the morning."

"Thanks, bro."

"Anytime. You know that. Want me to bring Jeb, too?"

"No, I think you and I can handle it. Dylan should be back any day now, too. And Trish. If we need backup, they can step in."

"What kind of backup are we talking about?" Tyler asked.

"Not the six-shooter variety," Michael said with the first genuine laugh he'd uttered in days.

"I'm relieved. Just remember one thing till I get there."

"What's that?"

"There's nothing a Delacourt can't do, once he puts his mind to it. Get more than one of us in a room and we're indomitable."

"I hope so," Michael said fervently. "For once in my life I'm counting on it."

He wasn't sure when he said it if he was thinking of Josh and Jamie, or if he was thinking about Grace.

# Chapter Ten

Grace tossed and turned for what seemed like hours before finally giving up, tugging on her robe and padding down the hall to the bathroom to get herself a glass of water. On her way she spotted a light on downstairs and opted to head to the kitchen instead.

Was Michael still up? Was one of the boys sick? She peeked into Josh and Jamie's room, saw that they were both sound asleep, then headed for the stairs. It had to be Michael.

She crept down silently, then peered into the living room. He was stretched out in an oversized chair in front of a fire that was little more than burning embers. He was holding a half-empty glass of wine in one hand, but his eyes were closed. She inched closer, intending only to throw an afghan over him and take away the precariously balanced glass, but he opened his eyes as she neared.

"What are you doing up?" he asked, his gaze settling on the deep *V* of her robe.

Grace barely resisted the urge to tug the robe closed. She was not going to let him see that he could make her nervous with nothing more than a glance. "I couldn't sleep," she told him. "What about you? Have you even been to bed?"

He shook his head. "Come over here and sit with me," he suggested. When she didn't move, he added quietly, "Please."

She wanted to. Oh, how she wanted to throw caution to the wind and slide into his embrace, but were want and need enough? "Why?" she asked, her gaze locked with his.

A smile tugged at his lips. "Just because," he said lightly.

She shook her head. "Not good enough."

"Because I need you, Grace," he said, his voice raw. "There, you got me to say it. Is that enough?"

Was it? Whether it was or not, she was drawn across the room until she was standing beside him. Still, she didn't join him in the chair. Watching her intently, he held out his hand.

The instant she put her hand in his, she knew that the choice had been made. This was the man she had loved for as long as she could remember. This was the man whose slightest touch was magical. Even now, with hands clasped and nothing more, she felt the heat and tension building inside, felt her pulse ricochet wildly. Six years and nothing had changed.

He still had the power to make her weak-kneed with longing.

His thumb rested on her wrist. There was a glint of satisfaction in his eyes as he detected her racing pulse. "Come on, Gracie," he urged, using the nickname only he had ever dared. "One more step."

One step, she thought. It sounded so insignificant, and yet it would change everything. It would put her back in Michael's arms, leave her vulnerable and aching and needy. And even if she satisfied that need tonight or tomorrow or the next day, in the end she would be alone again. How could she do that to herself, open herself to that kind of pain?

As she debated with herself, he waited, exhibiting more patience than usual. In the end, that was what convinced her. She had the sense that he would wait forever, if need be. She found that somehow reassuring.

With a sigh, she settled in his lap, snuggled against his chest in a way that had once been as familiar to her as the rasp of his five o'clock shadow against her skin. His cheeks were shadowed now by the beginnings of a beard. With hesitant fingertips, she caressed the very masculine, sandpaper texture, then drifted lower to rest her hand against the heat of his neck.

All the while his eyes glittered, darkened with some emotion she couldn't quite read.

"It's not going to be enough," he said at last. "I thought it might be, but it's not. I want you, Gracie. All of you."

She had accepted that before taking that first step, so the words came as no shock, but the shudder of anticipation did. "I know," she replied softly. "I don't think a day has gone by that I haven't wanted you. Not in six years."

He regarded her with apparent amazement. "Seriously?"

"Have you ever known me to kid around about something like that?"

A smug grin tugged at the corners of his mouth. "So that's why you've been so tough on me whenever you had the opportunity? Sexual frustration?"

She scowled at his assessment, started to pull away, but he held her in place with little effort.

"Don't go," he said.

"Why should I stay?"

"Because you want to," he suggested lightly. "And because I need you to."

She sighed. "Oh, Michael, I wish you wouldn't say things like that."

"Why?"

"Because they confuse me."

"I thought I was being straightforward and honest." He took her hand and moved it to the hard shaft pressing against her. "Here's the evidence, counselor."

"But that's just it," she said. "You and I have different definitions of need, different expectations."

His gaze settled on her breasts. The nipples were pushing against the silky fabric of her robe. "Are you so sure of that?"

"It's not all about sex," she said impatiently. "If it were, I would have stayed with you years ago. You and I never had any problems in bed. All it took was a glance for us to be ready, a touch. I found it maddening that I could be so furious with you, so sure that I had to get you out of my life, and yet my body would betray me, just as it's doing now.''

''Are you so sure it's a betrayal?'' he asked. ''Maybe it's just reminding you of something that's right, something that never should have ended.''

''It had to end, Michael. You know it did. You weren't ready to make the kind of commitment I needed, the kind I still need. I have to know I can count on a man, that he's going to be there for me when it's important, not tied up in some endless, insignificant meeting. I need to know that *I'm* not insignificant.''

''The future doesn't come with guarantees. Isn't it enough that *I'm* here now?''

''You're only here because you were tricked into coming, because you found two scared boys in the barn and you're too honorable to desert them. Tell me you're not chomping at the bit to be back in Houston, back in your office with a schedule of back-to-back meetings and nonstop phone calls.''

He hesitated, which was answer enough. Then, to her surprise, he said, ''I'm not. I was before you got here, but I'm not now. I've never been less bored in my life.''

''It's been a couple of days,'' she scoffed. ''How long do you really think that will last? You're a compulsive overachiever.''

''You're not the first person to say that to me recently.''

She couldn't help smiling at his irritated expression. ''Tyler, I presume?''

''Exactly. He's never let me forget that I've done

a lot of stupid things in my life because of work— or that the worst one was missing your graduation.''

''Since the message obviously hasn't sunk in, apparently he hasn't said it often enough.''

''Who says it hasn't sunk in?'' he protested. ''I learn from my mistakes.''

''Then why haven't you had a serious relationship in all these years?'' she asked bluntly. ''And don't try telling me it's because you couldn't get me out of your head. I know better. I read the society pages. There's been a steady stream of beautiful women in your life, but none of them lasted more than a few weeks.''

He regarded her with smug amusement. ''Interesting.''

''What?''

''That you followed my love life so closely.''

''The Houston media followed it closely. It was hard for anyone who reads the newspaper to miss. Based on what I read, I'd be willing to bet that sooner or later you got tied up in this or that and just forgot all about the lady of the moment. The next time you surfaced, you just moved on to someone new, probably because the last lover wouldn't take you back. Or maybe because by then you'd forgotten her name.''

He winced at the harsh assessment, but he didn't deny it. At last, sounding wounded, he asked, ''Is that what you really think? Do you honestly think I'm that cavalier about women?''

''Aren't you?''

''No. I wasn't cavalier about you, either. I made a mistake. A bad one. But I never stopped loving you. You threw me out, remember? You weighed everything we had against that one mistake and dumped me.''

Grace thought she detected hurt in his eyes to match the wounded tone in his voice, even after all this time, but surely that couldn't be, surely she'd never had that much power over him. It was true that it had been one mistake—one huge mistake in her eyes—but there had been signs it would happen again and again.

"You know why I did it," she said.

"I know what you said. I even know what you believe, but I think it was something else entirely, Gracie."

She stared at him in astonishment. "Such as?"

"I think you were scared, maybe even more terrified than I was. I think I gave you the perfect excuse to run and hide behind old fears." His gaze locked on hers. "Well? Am I right?"

"I…" Her voice faltered. Not once had she ever considered that she had seized on a mistake to bail out of a relationship that she feared would end down the road anyway. Had being abandoned by her father made her instinctively distrust Michael—any man— right from the start? Although she didn't like what it said about her level of insecurity, she couldn't deny the possibility. If she'd given him a chance to prove himself back then, would Michael have changed or would he have let her down? She hadn't wanted to find out.

"Maybe," she finally conceded.

He gave a nod of satisfaction. "Now we're getting somewhere."

He seemed so pleased, but she was more confused than ever. "Where?"

"Out of the past and into the present," he said. "How about it? Can we start here and now and see where it leads us?"

She stood up to move away from him, because when she was in his arms, she obviously couldn't think straight.

"This isn't the time for this," she said, gesturing vaguely toward the stairs. "The boys—"

"Are a separate issue," he said firmly. "This is about you and me. Are you willing to give us another chance? Or are you still too scared to try?"

Panic welled up inside her. She wanted to seize the opportunity he was dangling in front of her, but how could she when Josh and Jamie's fate needed to be decided? Or was that just another convenient excuse to avoid risking her heart?

"I don't know," she whispered. Then, because the temptation was so powerful, she added, "Maybe."

As if he sensed her struggle and that the concession she was making might be the best she could do, he smiled. "'Maybe' is good enough for now. Go on upstairs and get some sleep, Grace. Tomorrow's going to be a difficult day."

Surprised that he'd let her off the hook so easily, she nodded. "Are you coming?"

"Are you inviting me to share your bed?"

"No."

"I thought not. You go on. I'll be up soon."

She started away, but his voice stopped her.

"Gracie, you don't have to lock your door. I can

take no for an answer. I won't sneak in and ravish you."

She chuckled despite herself. "Too bad. It's been a long time since I've been ravished."

His heated gaze sent desire flaming through her.

"Just say the word and I can change that," he said.

"I'll keep that in mind." In fact, she thought it was likely that she would think about very little else.

Michael's blood was pumping fast and furiously as he watched Grace go upstairs. A part of him cursed the fact that he'd let her get away. He knew if he'd kissed her, if he'd caressed her, even innocently, he could have persuaded her to make love with him. Then he wouldn't be sitting here in this aching, aroused state, regretting the fact that he had a sense of decency and honor.

She'd been right, though, this was not the time to start something, not with her emotions running high because of Josh and Jamie. He would have been taking advantage of that, using her vulnerability to get her to turn to him for more than emotional support.

He waited for an hour after she'd left him before he too climbed the stairs and made his way to bed. He very nearly paused outside her door and reached for the knob—just to check on her, he told himself—but then he remembered his promise. He moved on to his own room and slid between the icy sheets, once more cursing the fact that he could have had her there to warm them.

He fell into a restless sleep, tormented by dreams in which Grace turned her back on him over and over. By the time he awoke, he was miserable and out of sorts.

A cold shower revived him somewhat. Years of forcing himself to stay focused on the task at hand got him down the stairs in a reasonable mood, ready to tackle their predicament with Josh and Jamie.

Grace barely looked at him, but he noticed she'd abandoned her more provocative shorts and tank tops for slacks and a sedate blouse. Was that for his benefit, a way to warn him off, perhaps? Or preparation for the meeting with Justin?

Jamie looked up from his plate of scrambled eggs and bacon, glanced from Michael to Grace and back again. His fork hit the plate with a clatter. "Okay, what's up? You guys have been acting all weird since we went to town yesterday."

"Everything is fine," Michael began, only to have Grace interrupt.

"We need to tell them," she said, putting a plate in front of him with a thump, then taking her own place at the table.

Michael noticed she didn't touch her food. It was evident that she, too, had lost her appetite, just as Jamie had. Even Josh was merely stirring his food around on his plate, not eating it.

"Tell us what?" Jamie asked.

"Michael and I have made a decision," she began, looking to him for help.

"Right." He searched for a way to put it into words without scaring them half to death.

Jamie shoved his chair back from the table so fast, it tilted over and crashed to the floor. "You promised," he said, his voice quivering with outrage and betrayal as he stared at Grace. "You told me you wouldn't decide anything unless me and Josh said so, too."

"Hold it," Michael said. "Don't go yelling at Grace. She's on your side. We both are."

"Yeah, but you're just like all grown-ups. You make the decisions, then we're supposed to go along with them, right? Well, not this time. Me and Josh are out of here. Come on, Josh."

Josh's eyes had filled with tears during the exchange. "But I don't want to go."

"Didn't you hear them?" Jamie said, exasperated. "They're deciding what to do with us. They just want us to go along with it."

"But they haven't said what it is yct," Josh said reasonably. "I want to hear."

"Please, Jamie," Grace said gently. "Let us explain at least."

He regarded her with obvious misery and distrust. "Why should I?"

"Because I love you," she said simply.

The response clearly took him by surprise. "You do?"

The mix of distrust and hope in his voice almost broke Michael's heart.

"We both do," she said firmly. "That's why this is so important. I would never, ever do anything that I thought would hurt you or go against your best interests. Please believe that."

Jamie seemed to be struggling with himself, but eventually he righted his chair and sat in it. "Okay, I'll listen, but if I don't like it, Josh and me are out of here."

"Fair enough," Grace said.

Before she could say anything, Michael heard a key turning in the front door, then Tyler's shouted greeting from the foyer.

"Who's that?" Jamie asked suspiciously. He was halfway out of his chair again, ready to bolt.

"Settle down," Michael said. "It's my brother."

Grace regarded him with surprise. "Tyler's here?"

Michael nodded. "I called him last night before you came downstairs."

"And of course I came running to the rescue," Tyler said, strolling into the kitchen and pausing to drop a kiss on Grace's cheek. "Good to see you again, Grace."

"You, too," she said, standing. "Are you hungry? I can fix you something."

"Have you ever known Tyler not to be hungry?" Michael asked, but he regarded his brother with gratitude. "Thanks for getting here so fast."

Jamie had settled back in his seat, but his gaze remained wary.

"You guys don't look like brothers," Josh said.

Tyler grinned. "That's 'cause he's so ugly, right? I'm the handsome one."

"You got hair like ours, blond," Josh said, ignoring Tyler's claim. "Michael's is real dark. And you got lots of muscles. You must work out a lot."

"Tyler works in the oil fields every chance he gets," Michael corrected.

"Cool," Jamie said, his reserved facade slipping for a minute. "Is it fun?"

"You bet," Tyler told him, dragging a fifth chair up to the table and sliding it in next to Jamie. "Some people," he said with a pointed glance at Michael, "don't like to get dirty. They just want to sit in a fancy office and reap the rewards of all my hard work."

"Somebody has to sell that crude or it's a waste of time bringing it in," Michael reminded him in what was an old argument. Of course, usually the debate took place between Tyler and their father and it usually was conducted with a whole lot more rancor.

"Old turf," Tyler said, winking at Grace when she put a plate in front of him. "Isn't it?"

"I've been hearing it as far back as I can recall," she agreed. "What amazes me is that you haven't bolted for a rival oil company, where you won't have to fight to do the job you love."

Tyler gave an exaggerated shudder. "Not even I am that brave. I'm not sure Dad's heart is strong enough to take it and I don't want to be the one who puts him in his grave."

He put down his fork and turned to Jamie. "Okay, enough about my career choices. Tell me about you."

"I'm Jamie."

"And I'm Josh."

"I heard you were hiding out in the barn when my brother found you. What's the deal?"

As if they instinctively trusted Tyler, both boys began spilling the events of the last few days before finally winding down.

"So today *we're* gonna decide what happens to us," Jamie concluded with a pointed look at Michael.

"We were just about to discuss it when you came in," Michael said.

"What's the plan?"

"Michael wants to call Justin Adams. It's been suggested he would be a very good ally," Grace said, pointedly not mentioning that Justin was the sheriff.

Tyler shot a look at Michael. "Do you think that's wise?"

"Dylan trusts him."

Satisfied by their brother's approval, Tyler nodded. "Okay. Then what?"

"We see what he has to say."

His brother looked as if he wanted to ask more, but instead he fell silent.

"Tyler, do you disagree?" Grace asked

"Not exactly," he said slowly. "Have you come up with a best-case scenario, something to give Justin to work with?"

Michael exchanged a look with Grace, then nodded. "Grace wants to take the boys to live with her."

Jamie and Josh whirled on her and stared, wide-eyed. "You mean it?" Jamie asked incredulously.

"I mean it," she said firmly, then cautioned, "Don't get your hopes up, though. There's no guarantee we can pull it off."

"You will," Josh said, scrambling from his chair to give her a fierce hug. "I know you will."

Grace looked at Jamie, who hadn't budged. "Is this okay with you, Jamie?"

Blinking back tears, the boy nodded. Grace held out her hand, and after a slight hesitation, Jamie put his into it.

"Deal," he said in a voice choked with emotion.

Michael felt the salty sting of tears in his own eyes as he watched the three of them, already united, already a family in their own eyes.

But where the hell did that leave him?

Tyler caught his gaze, gave him a sympathetic look before saying, "Hey, Grace, why don't you and the boys take off for a while? Leave the cleanup for Michael and me."

She stared at him, clearly flabbergasted by the offer. "You don't have to ask me twice," she said, then glanced in Michael's direction. "Of course, it might almost be worth it to stick around and see how you look in an apron."

"If you can find one with frills, I'll take a picture," Tyler offered, grinning.

Michael scowled with mock ferocity. "Thanks, bro."

"Get out of here, Grace," Tyler encouraged. "You don't want to stick around for the bloodshed."

She grinned at him. "Come on, kids. Let's take advantage of this magnanimous offer and go out to see the horses."

"Can we ride?" Josh begged.

"Not without Slade here," she said.

Surprisingly, her decision didn't draw a whiff of protest. Apparently the boys had no intention of risking her wrath when she was willing to be their new mom.

After they'd gone, Tyler turned to Michael. "When you want something as badly as you obviously want those three, you fight for it," he advised mildly.

"Don't even go there," Michael retorted.

''You're talking to me,'' Tyler said. ''Don't waste your breath trying to deny it. You've never gotten over Grace. And I've never seen you take to a couple of kids the way you've obviously taken to those two. What are you going to do about it?''

''Besides begging Grace for another chance?'' Michael said wryly. ''I've already done that.''

''Did she turn you down?''

''She said maybe.''

''Then I guess you're just going to have to be more persuasive,'' Tyler said. ''Because I don't want to think that my brother is an idiot. Besides, Delacourts never fail. Isn't that the lesson Dad started drilling into us when we were still in our cradles?''

''Grace refuses to so much as discuss our future until we've protected Jamie and Josh from being separated again.''

''Then get Justin over here and get the ball rolling,'' Tyler said.

''Good advice,'' Michael agreed. ''Mind telling me what we do if it starts careening downhill?''

''We pull out the big guns,'' Tyler said readily.

''Oh?''

''Dad and Harlan Adams. I can't imagine a bureaucrat anywhere who wouldn't quake in his boots at the sight of those two formidable men.''

Michael took heart at the suggestion. It was true. Nobody he knew would dare to say no to his father or to Harlan Adams, and no two men were more fiercely committed to the concept of family. With them on her side, Josh and Jamie were as good as Grace's.

Once again, though, he had to ask himself: Where did that leave him?

## Chapter Eleven

Grace stood at the fence to the corral and watched as Jamie and Josh groomed the two horses that were their favorites. Slade had taught them well. They were thorough, murmuring to the horses the whole time and drawing gentle nudges at their pockets where both had stored pieces of apple.

"Stop it," Jamie said, laughing when one curious nudge almost landed him on his backside in the dirt. "You'll get your treat when I'm done."

The horse whinnied in response, clearly unhappy about being put off. Jamie finally gave a resigned shrug and pulled out a chunk of apple, then held it out in his open palm. The horse took it daintily, but seconds later the filly was back for more.

"If I keep feeding you, you're going to be too fat to gallop," Jamie chided her.

The horse's only response was to try to burrow her nose into his pocket.

Grace laughed at their war of wills. She prayed that life could go on being like this for Jamie, simple and uncomplicated after years of having too many worries on his young shoulders. He'd been barely older than Josh was now when he'd concluded it was up to him to see that he and his brother were reunited for their birthdays, no matter what the system did to separate them.

She thought about her plan to take them back to Houston with her. It was evident that both boys were eager to go, but was it right to take them away from this ranching world they so obviously adored, where in just a few days they had begun to flourish?

She was still troubled by that when Michael eased up behind her and put his hands on either side of the corral fence, effectively trapping her body against the hard planes of his. A shiver of anticipation skittered over her at the intimate contact.

"They look as if they're in their element," Michael observed.

"Don't they?" She turned to look up at him. "What if I'm doing the wrong thing?"

He regarded her with surprise. "Meaning?"

"Maybe I shouldn't take them away from here. Maybe I should let Sharon Lynn or one of the others around here make a home for them. They'd have friends, fresh air, horses."

"Sweetheart, you'll bring even more to their lives. Besides, we don't even know if Sharon Lynn was able to convince Cord to take them in."

"She will," Grace said with confidence. "Or

she'll get one of the other Adamses to agree. Look at them. They're so happy, probably happier than they've ever been.''

"Don't you think that's as much because they're together as it is because they're on a ranch?''

"I don't know that for sure," she said candidly. "Shouldn't I give them the option?''

"We don't even know if that option exists," Michael reminded her again. "Let's leave things as they are. You love those boys. You can give them a good life. More important, you *want* to give them a good life. If they need horses to be happy, you'll find a way to see that they have them. My guess is all they really need is a home and you.''

Her gaze met his. His reassurance meant the world to her, ironically because she knew he wouldn't let emotion overrule his clear-eyed objectivity. "Thank you for saying that.''

"I meant it." He caressed her cheek. "It's all I would need.''

She didn't know what to say to that. He grinned at her silence.

"Left you speechless? That has to be a first.''

"I can't think about that now," she told him honestly. "I just can't.''

"I know. I'm not pressing you for an answer, just reminding you that the issue is on the table.''

She smiled. "I'm not likely to forget that." Her smile faltered then. "What about Justin? Did you call him?''

Michael nodded. "He's on his way.''

"Maybe we should warn the boys that he's a sheriff. If he comes in here in a cop car and wearing a uniform, they might panic.''

''Which is why Tyler's coming out any second to take them into town,'' Michael said. ''There's no need to get them worked up unnecessarily.''

As if on cue, Tyler came out of the house and called to the boys, ''Hey, guys, how about riding into town with me? I could use some help.''

Both boys hesitated. ''What kind of help?''

''Getting there, for starters. You probably know the way better than I do,'' he said in what was clearly a blatant lie. ''And my brother has given me this endless list of things to pick up. I'll never be able to carry them all myself.''

''I guess we could go,'' Jamie said. He glanced at Grace. ''Is it okay? If that guy's coming over to talk about us, shouldn't we get to stay?''

''We've agreed on our plan. We won't change it without talking it over with you. In the meantime, a trip into town sounds great to me.''

''How come you're not going?'' Josh asked.

''Because they've got to wait for this Justin person,'' Jamie said. ''And they want us out of the way.''

''You're too smart for your own good,'' Michael told him, ruffling his hair. ''Now scoot.'' He bent down to whisper, ''And make sure he buys you pizza and ice cream. Play your cards right and he might take you to the toy store, too.''

''All right,'' Josh enthused, easily won over.

Five minutes after the three of them had driven off, Grace heard what had to be the sheriff's cruiser coming through the thick stand of pines between the house and the road.

"I'm not sure I'm ready for this," she admitted to Michael.

"Sure you are. Just remember that I'm right here beside you and I'm not going anywhere. Work your charm and your legal magic on him."

Justin exited the car and strolled toward them wearing his crisply ironed uniform and sunglasses that shaded his eyes and left his expression enigmatic. Grace hated not being able to see behind those lenses to gauge his reaction. She thought she knew one way to assure they'd come off.

"Hello," she said briskly, holding out her hand. "I'm Grace Foster, an attorney from Houston. Why don't we go inside and have a glass of iced tea? It's getting warm out here."

"Fine by me," Justin agreed, then turned to shake Michael's hand. "Good to see you again. It's been a long time."

"I know. I don't get over to see my sister and brother nearly enough."

"So they say," Justin said, then chuckled. "Hear they tricked you into coming this time, then ran off and left you to fend for yourself."

Michael gave him a rueful grin. "Don't remind me."

Inside, as expected, Justin removed his sunglasses, but he didn't sit down. He leaned against the counter and waited for her to begin. Grace had dealt with plenty of law enforcement officers in her time. She never let them get the better of her, but now, with so much at stake, she had to struggle against panic.

"How much do you know?" she asked him, gazing into penetrating blue eyes that she imagined could intimidate a suspect in nothing flat. She almost regretted getting him to remove the sunglasses.

"Sharon Lynn filled us in last night. To tell you the truth I expected a call before now."

"We...I...had some thinking to do," Grace said.

"About?"

"My own role in all of this."

Justin waited patiently.

"I want Jamie and Josh to come live with me. I don't want them separated again."

Justin's gaze registered surprise. "I was under the impression you were hoping someone around here might take them in. Sharon Lynn and Cord are considering it."

"I know, but since I talked with her, I've given it a lot of thought. They're great kids. I can give them a good home. Jamie and Josh have agreed. I want to get the ball rolling to see that that's what happens.

Justin regarded her with concern. "You've talked this over with them? What if you can't make it happen? They'll be devastated."

"I made them a promise that they would have a say," she said defensively. "I kept that promise."

"And if the court turns down your request?" Justin asked. "What then?"

"That won't happen," Michael said at once. His gaze met Justin's evenly. "Will it?"

Justin didn't flinch under the intensity of that look. "You know that that's beyond my control."

"Maybe so, but it'll go a long way toward putting the court on Grace's side if you can report that the

boys are happy with her and forget about the fact
that she kept their presence here a secret for a few
days while we sorted things out."

"In other words, you want me to fudge the truth,"
Justin said.

"For the good of those two boys," Michael
stressed.

Justin didn't look one bit happy about the request,
but eventually he gave a curt nod. "Let me start
making some calls. Try to salvage this situation as
best I can." His piercing gaze landed on Grace.
"You and I could both land in a heap of trouble for
this. If everybody just grabbed up any stray kid they
saw and took them home, we'd have chaos. There's
a reason for all the rules and regulations, you know."

"I do know, which is why I'm so grateful to you,"
she said. "Believe me, when you meet Josh and Jamie, you'll see that they're worth the risk."

"If Sharon Lynn hadn't already told me that, I
wouldn't be doing this," he said succinctly. He
grinned ruefully. "That, combined with the fact that
I'm under orders from Grandpa Harlan to take care
of this in a way that protects those brothers from
being separated. My grandfather gets his dander up
at the slightest hint that some adult isn't doing everything possible to give a child the best possible
family. He's chomping at the bit to get over here and
meet these two, but Janet's trying her best to keep
him at White Pines and out of the middle of things."

He shook his head. "I could tell her she's fighting
a losing battle, but why waste my breath. She knows
it anyway. And just so you know, she also pulled me
aside to tell me if you need another legal mind on

this to give her a call. Given your intention to ask for custody of those boys, you might consider it. You won't find a better advocate than Janet.''

''I appreciate the offer,'' Grace said sincerely. ''And I may do that before we're done. It probably isn't all that smart for me to represent myself.''

She held up the pitcher. ''More tea before you make those calls?''

''No, thanks. I'm fine.''

''Then I'll show you to Trish's office,'' Michael offered. ''You can make your calls from there.''

After the two men had left the room, Grace finally felt the knot of tension in her stomach ease. Justin Adams might be a law-and-order, by-the-book sheriff, but he was a good man. Dylan had been right about that and she could see the kindness in his eyes. It was a good thing, since not only her future, but Jamie's and Josh's, were all in his hands.

''I hate standing on the sidelines while someone else gets things done. What do you think is happening in there?'' Grace asked Michael when Justin hadn't come back to the kitchen after an hour.

''I think he's doing everything he can to make sure this turns out the way we want it to.''

He stood behind her chair and massaged her shoulders, finally feeling them begin to relax beneath his touch. Unfortunately, the contact was having the opposite effect on him. He felt as if he were grasping a live wire. There were sparks detonating inside him. Memories exaggerated them into full-fledged passion and left him aching with need.

He cursed this inability he had to control himself

around her. Desire wasn't what Grace needed now. She needed moral support, compassion, maybe even financial backing should her resources be more limited than he imagined them to be. She didn't need lust.

She glanced up at him, surprising him with a grin. "Nice distraction," she teased.

"Is it?" he asked.

And then, because he could no longer resist, he bent down and covered her lips with his. White-hot urgency slammed through him, making his blood roar. Damned, if he didn't think it made his teeth tingle, too. He was sure if Grace looked into his eyes, she would be terrified by the hunger she saw there.

With a shudder, with a last probe of tongue against tongue, he pulled back, sucked in a deep, calming breath, but he didn't take his hands from her shoulders. He wasn't feeling that generous. He craved the contact, any contact that would remind her, remind both of them of all that was at stake.

"Even better than the last distraction," she murmured. "But risky. I want to be here, not upstairs in bed when Justin's through making his calls."

Michael took heart from the implication that he could lure her to bed with a few more potent kisses. "Hold that thought," he suggested. "In the meantime, how about playing cards or working on a puzzle? Knowing Trish, there must be some around here somewhere."

In the past, when things had been good between him and Grace, there had always been a thousand-piece jigsaw puzzle set up for rainy afternoons. He'd been surprised by how much he enjoyed the quiet activity, but he suspected that had more to do with his companion and the sneaky distraction of her foot against his calf under the table than the challenge of the puzzle. She also played a cutthroat game of rummy.

Although her anxious gaze remained firmly fixed on the door, she nodded. "That would be nice."

Michael checked a few cupboards and finally found some playing cards. "Rummy okay?"

"Sure."

He dealt the cards, but she was slow to pick up her hand.

"What could be taking so long?" she asked.

"He's just being thorough. It doesn't mean there's anything wrong."

"I hope you're right."

"Watching for him won't bring him back here any faster. Pick up your cards. Otherwise, I'm going to win by default, and I have some fascinating ideas about what my prize should be."

That caught her attention. "Oh, really?" she said, snatching up her hand and studying it with fierce concentration. "You haven't got a chance, buster."

He grinned. "Is that so?"

As he'd anticipated, within minutes, she was thoroughly caught up in the game and happily taking him to the cleaners. When she'd slapped down another winning hand, she regarded him with a triumphant expression.

"Any questions about who's the grand champion?" she asked.

"Maybe I'm just letting you win to keep your mind off of Justin," he suggested.

"Letting me win?" she retorted indignantly. "I don't think so."

"You'll never know for sure, will you?"

She picked up the cards and shuffled. "Okay, that's it. This is war." She placed the cards down on the table with a snap. "Winner take all."

"An interesting bet," he agreed. "Since we're not playing for money, what does it mean exactly?"

Her expression turned thoughtful. "Okay, here it is. It means that if I win this hand, you will agree to one whole month of working nine to five, Monday to Friday, and no more. And just so you know, the month doesn't begin until you are actually back in Houston and back at work."

He started to protest that he didn't have a nine-to-five job, but that was her point, of course. She wanted to see if he could do it, if he'd learned anything at all about putting his priorities in order. He vowed to prove he could, even if he won the hand.

"Agreed," he said, clearly startling her with his ready acceptance of the terms. "And if I win—"

"You won't."

He scowled at her with mock ferocity. "*When* I win, you and Josh and Jamie will let me court you."

Color flared in her cheeks at the suggestion. "Excuse me? You plan to court all three of us?"

"After this is settled, you'll be a package deal, correct?"

"Yes."

"Then me courting you will also affect them."

"I suppose," she said as if she suspected there were a trick in there she hadn't quite discerned.

"Agreed?"

She nodded finally. "Agreed."

Michael looked at his cards then and had to bite back the urge to utter a whoop of triumph. She had dealt him a near-perfect hand. One card was all he needed for victory. He drew his first card, stared at it, then snuggled it into place in his hand.

He glanced across the table, caught the wary expression in her eyes and was about to place the winning hand down on the table, when Justin stepped into the room.

"Okay," he said, his expression grim. "Here's the deal."

Grace was immediately on her feet, all thoughts of the card game clearly abandoned. "Tell me."

"Sit, sweetheart," Michael urged, drawing her back to the table. "Give the man a chance."

Justin pulled up a chair and sat opposite her. "After some grumbling about people taking the law into their own hands, obstructing justice, etcetera, the authorities are willing to overlook all of that and leave Jamie and Josh in your care until a hearing can be set."

Grace uttered a sigh of relief.

"Hang on. That's only the beginning," Justin warned. "In the meantime, if you want to become their foster parent, you have to take the appropriate steps, file all the paperwork, go through the clearances. I'm sure you know the drill."

"Not a problem," Grace said. "I'll get started this afternoon."

He slid a piece of paper toward her. "Here's the fax number. I left the papers they've already faxed here for your signature on the desk in Trish's office.

Fill everything out and get it back to them before they close for the day. Otherwise, they're likely to be camping on the doorstep over here first thing in the morning."

"Is there any chance she won't be approved?" Michael asked.

She frowned at the question. "Why would you even suggest that they might turn me down?"

"Because I'm trying to be realistic here. I think we need to know if our failure to turn those kids in right away could affect the outcome of this."

"He's right," Justin said. "The social services worker on the case is just relieved that the boys are okay. So are the previous foster parents. Neither of those families has any intention of fighting to get Jamie or Josh back. But there's a supervisor in the office over there who's mad as hell. He likes to have all the *i*'s dotted and all the *t*'s crossed before the fact, not after. He won't cut you any slack, Grace."

"Name?" Michael asked.

Justin glanced at his notes. "Franklin Oakley. He's been around a long time. Runs a tight ship. The caseworker says he's the kind to hold a grudge. Worse, he really hates lawyers. Thinks they're the scourge of the system. 'Bunch of damn bleeding hearts' is the exact quote."

Grace looked shaken. "Terrific."

"Don't panic. We'll take care of Mr. Oakley," Michael said quietly.

"How?"

"There are ways."

"Delacourt or Adams influence won't cut it," Justin warned. "If anything, it'll just infuriate him. You know the type. They hate anything that smacks of undue influence, and they especially hate the wealthy and powerful.''

''That won't matter if he's no longer in a position to do any harm,'' Michael retorted.

Grace regarded him with a shocked expression. ''Michael, you can't get the man fired.''

''I can, if that's what it takes,'' he said coldly.

''Let's not resort to that just yet,'' she pleaded. ''Let's just play by the rules.''

He wanted to warn her that playing by the rules might cost her Jamie and Josh, but this was her call. He had to do it her way. ''Okay,'' he said at last. ''We'll try it your way. If things start turning sour, though, we do it mine. If Mr. Oakley had been doing his job right from the beginning, those boys would still be together somewhere. They wouldn't have had to run away in the first place.''

Grace still looked troubled, but she nodded. She faced Justin. ''Thank you. I know if I had made these calls myself, we wouldn't be where we are. I would probably have told Mr. Oakley some of the same things Michael just said. I owe you.''

''You don't owe me,'' Justin said. ''Just try not to break any more laws while you're in my jurisdiction.''

''Not a one,'' Grace vowed. ''We'll be model citizens.''

''Scout's honor,'' Michael said.

Grace stared at him. ''When were you a Scout?''

''Never. It just seemed like the thing to say.''

She rolled her eyes. ''I'll keep him in line,'' she promised Justin.

He chuckled. "That ought to be interesting to see. Sorry I can't stick around."

After he'd gone, Michael caught Grace's gaze. "So, you're going to keep me in line, are you? Just how do you intend to do that?"

"I have my ways," she said airily.

"Sounds promising. I'll be fascinated to see them in action."

She kept her gaze level for a moment, but then her glance fell. She caught sight of the cards lying on the table.

"Want to finish our game before I fill out this paperwork?" she asked.

"No need," he told her, spreading out his winning hand. "It's already over."

She stared at the cards in shock. "How can that be?"

"Just lucky, I guess."

"You cheated. You must have."

"No need, darlin'. You dealt the cards. I won. It's as simple as that. I think you wanted me to win."

"I most certainly did not."

"Well, the cards don't lie. I won, and now I aim to collect on my bet."

"How?" she asked warily.

"Don't look so terrified. If I do it right, courting's practically painless. You just have to get used to bouquets of flowers, the occasional box of candy, a little fine dining, maybe a kiss now and then."

"The boys will love that," she noted wryly.

"They can share in some of it, but the kisses are all yours," he clarified. "In fact, now might be a good time to collect on the first one. We're all alone. You're already looking a little flushed."

She waved the faxes at him. "I have forms to fill out."

"It's just one kiss, a sample of things to come."

"Oh, all right," she said with an exaggerated sigh of resignation. She puckered her lips and waited, eyes closed.

Michael regarded her with amusement, then gave her a gentle peck on the cheek that had her eyes snapping open.

"That's it?" she demanded.

"You wanted something more?"

"Of course not."

He chuckled. "Liar."

As she opened her mouth to tell yet another fib, he angled his head, swooped in and stole another kiss, this one packing the kind of wallop that left them both breathless.

"Now there's an incentive," he murmured.

"An incentive for what?"

"Who knows?" he teased. "A few more of those and I might get home from work every day for lunch."

## Chapter Twelve

The reality of what she was doing slammed into Grace as she was filling out the stack of papers Justin had received by fax. She had closeted herself in Trish's office, partly to get the necessary paperwork done, but just as much to get out of the path of Michael's devastating kisses. They left her confused and shaken and right now she definitely needed all her wits about her.

A tiny voice in her head shouted that she was making a totally impulsive decision, a decision driven by emotion. Grace Foster, tough, single-focus attorney, didn't do things like that. In fact, her clearheadedness was one of her most prized assets. So why this decision?

Because Jamie and Josh needed to be together.

They needed stability and love and she could give them both. Simple as that.

And twice as complicated, she thought ruefully. She was charging into this because she didn't see an alternative. And—she realized with sudden insight— because she needed them almost as much as they needed her. They filled a void in her life, an empty place in her heart. They promised something she hadn't had since she'd split up with Michael: love.

"It's the right thing to do," she murmured, trying to reassure herself. "Definitely the right thing."

She bent over the papers once more. A few minutes later she was just finishing the last form when she heard the thunder of feet hitting the porch. Shouts echoed through the house as Josh and Jamie came bolting inside, obviously exuberant after their trip into town. Their happiness reassured her. Hearing it, she was able to push aside the last, lingering doubts. She put the papers into the fax and sent them. Now all they had to do was wait.

And pray, she thought as she went to find the boys.

She found them in the kitchen raiding the refrigerator as if they were starved. Michael was observing the scene with apparent astonishment.

"Ty, I thought you were going to feed them in town," Michael said, watching them snatch up cheese and lunch meats for sandwiches.

"They're as voracious as a horde of locusts," Tyler declared. "I swear to you I bought them pizza— a large one with everything on it—and sundaes with the works, including double hot fudge. I don't understand where they put it."

Grace chuckled at his incredulous expression. "You don't remember being that age?"

"Of course I do, but we had our limits." He glanced at Michael. "Didn't we?"

"I certainly did," Michael retorted with a pious expression. "You, however, ate everything in sight, now that I think about it. No freshly baked cookie was safe with you in the house. We lost three housekeepers because they couldn't keep up with you."

Tyler shot him an exasperated look. "We did not. The only housekeeper who ever quit did so because you put a frog in her bed."

Josh and Jamie looked up at that, clearly fascinated.

"Cool," Jamie declared.

"Did you get punished?" Josh asked.

"Michael never got punished," Tyler said. "He was mother's favorite." He grinned. "Till Trish came along, anyway."

Michael groaned. "You are such a liar."

"Am not. You got away with murder, while the rest of us had to pay a heavy price for every little misdeed."

"What kind of price?" Josh asked, clearly fascinated.

"We were grounded, lost our TV privileges, had to clean our rooms. I'm telling you, our folks were tough."

"Get out the violins," Michael muttered.

Grace laughed. "Something tells me you are making every word of this up, Tyler Delacourt."

"He is," Michael assured her. "Except for his inability to get our father to leave him out in the oil fields, Tyler has gotten his way his entire life. The man was spoiled rotten. He was a skinny little thing, so the housekeepers always gave him the choicest food, the biggest servings of pie and cake. Every time I turned around Mother was bringing him another toy. He was the first one in the family to get his own computer.''

''Which you stole so you could run profit and loss statements on Delacourt Oil before you turned ten,'' Tyler countered.

''It must have been really cool living at your house,'' Jamie said quietly.

The observation brought a sudden halt to the teasing as the men clearly realized what a contrast their upbringing had been to Josh and Jamie's experiences. Not only had they been together, they had been surrounded by love and material things that Josh and Jamie could only dream about.

''It was cool,'' Michael told them. ''And once you're with Grace, it's going to be just as cool for you.''

Grace was startled that he would dangle that possibility out to them before it was a done deal. The less said about it until then, the better. ''Michael—''

''No, Grace, don't start doubting it. This is going to happen.''

''Things went okay with Justin, then?'' Tyler asked.

''Well enough,'' Grace conceded carefully.

Jamie's eyes registered concern. ''There's something you're not saying, isn't there?''

Grace shot an *I-told-you-so* look at Michael. ''They've agreed to let you stay with me for now.''

"All right!" Josh shouted.

"She said *for now,* dope. That's not forever," Jamie said.

"No, it's not forever," Grace admitted. "But it's a good start. We've got the ball rolling. We'll just have to wait and see what happens."

"How long do we have to wait?" Jamie asked.

"It's hard to tell. They'll set a hearing date, probably in a few days."

"But you're not giving up, right? Will we get to tell somebody what *we* want?"

"Maybe, down the road," she told him. "In the meantime, let's try not to worry about it."

"In fact, let's focus on something else," Michael told them. "I think I hear Slade. Are you guys ready for another riding lesson? I talked to him earlier, and I think he's going to take you on a real ride today."

"You mean, like, out of the corral?" Josh asked, eyes wide.

"Yep," Michael said. "He says you're ready and the horses are definitely eager for the exercise."

"Are you coming?" Jamie asked Michael. He was already heading for the door, sandwich in hand.

"Nope. I'll be out later to watch you guys. I want to talk to Grace for a bit."

"About us?"

Michael grinned at him. "Not everything is about you. In fact, if I could get my brother out of here, I might snatch a little time alone with Grace."

"So you can kiss her?" Josh wanted to know.

Grace felt the color rise in her cheeks. "There will be no kissing," she said in her haughtiest tone, but Michael only winked.

"Bet I can change her mind," he said.

Tyler dutifully stood up and followed Josh and Jamie to the door. He paused before leaving, though, and directed his own wink at Grace before facing his brother.

"Bet you can't."

"You're on," Michael responded at once.

As soon as they were alone, Grace scowled at Michael. "Hell will freeze over before you get another kiss from me, Michael Delacourt."

He merely grinned. "I love it when you get all huffy."

Exasperated, she started to leave the kitchen, but he snagged her hand. Despite herself, she felt a wave of anticipation wash over her.

"Michael—"

"Yes, Grace."

"I...will...not...kiss...you," she said emphatically. "Especially not so you can win some bet with your brother."

His gaze locked with hers. "How about because it's been a couple of hours since the last one and I don't think I can last another minute?"

Unfortunately, that echoed her own longing. "Maybe," she said. "Keep talking."

"How about because you drive me wild?"

"Better."

"How about because kissing you is the best thing that's happened to me in six years?"

She sighed and stepped closer, tilting her face up. "Me, too," she whispered, slowly opening her mouth to the tantalizing invasion of his tongue.

"Oh, yes," she murmured sometime later. "Definitely, me, too."

When Michael eventually went outside in search of the boys, Grace headed straight for the sink and a splash of cold water to cool off her suddenly over-active hormones. She was still standing there wondering how her life had taken this unexpected twist in such a short time when the doorbell rang.

Wondering who on earth it could be, she opened it to find a distinguished-looking white-haired gentleman on the porch. Even though he was dressed in the worn jeans and chambray shirt of a rancher, there was no mistaking that this was no ordinary rancher. She guessed at once that this was the indomitable Harlan Adams. Who else would have the audacity to drop in on strangers out of the blue?

"You must be Grace Foster," he said, extending his hand. He enfolded her hand in a powerful grip. Gaze steady and filled with curiosity, he surveyed her from head to toe. "Even prettier than I'd been told."

She grinned. "Thank you. You're as charming as *I've* been told."

"So the grandkids have been blabbing about me again," he said with a resigned expression. "Told all sorts of tales, no doubt. Don't believe 'em. I'm not half as bad as they say."

"I suppose that depends on your point of view, Mr. Adams."

"Call me Harlan. Or Grandpa Harlan, if it suits you better. Mind if I come in and sit a spell?" He gave an impatient wave of his cane. "Blasted knee's not what it once was, so they make me use this thing.

It's a damned nuisance, but what can I do? It puts Janet's mind at ease.''

"I'm sure your wife appreciates your thoughtfulness," she said, leading the way into the kitchen.

"Sometimes she does," he agreed as he sat down heavily. "Sometimes she doesn't quite see it the same way I do.''

Grace chuckled. "You mean even after all these years, you two haven't worked out all the kinks in your marriage?''

"Gracious, no. If we had, we'd just have to dream up new ones. Have to keep things lively.''

Grace offered him some iced tea, but he opted for coffee instead. "If it's not too much trouble.''

"Of course not.''

He regarded her with a satisfied smile that had her worrying. "Are you supposed to drink coffee?'' she asked as a scoop hovered over the coffeemaker. "I noticed there's decaf here, too.''

"Decaf's a waste of time. I like the real thing.''

She regarded him evenly. "Which isn't an answer at all.''

"Oh, for goodness sakes. It's one little cup of coffee. No need to make a big deal about it.''

Rather than argue, she made it weak. "Something tells me you're a sneaky man, Mr. Adams.''

"I am, and proud of it," he declared, snatching the cup of coffee before she could change her mind. He took a sip, then made a face. "No *oompf.*''

"Precisely what I intended," she retorted, thoroughly enjoying him. "Now why don't you tell me why you're here? I don't imagine you came all this way just to sneak a cup of coffee.''

"Came to meet those boys, of course. And you. I like to know what's going on around these parts, especially with family."

"Family?" she questioned, surprised by the claimed connection.

"Hardy works for me. I rent that bookstore space to Trish. Had a hand in getting the two of them together. That's close enough to being family for me."

"I see. So you've claimed Michael as well."

"He's Trish's brother, isn't he? Of course I do." He winked at her. "We'll have to see about you." He tapped his coffee cup. "You've got promise, though."

"Thank you, I think."

"Justin help you out with this situation?"

"He did."

"Anything I can do?"

"Not at the moment. He was able to get the authorities to agree to let me keep Josh and Jamie for the time being, while the rest is worked out."

"They'd have a good home with Sharon Lynn and Cody," he said. "She seems inclined to offer."

"I know and I appreciate it. I really do, but I'm thinking that they ought to stay with me."

"They'd have two parents here," he countered. "You and that young man gonna offer them that?"

She stared at him. "Michael? And me?"

"You know any other young men around here?"

"We're not...I mean, there's been no talk of anything permanent happening between Michael and me. We're just friends."

"Too bad. From what I've heard, those two boys could use a stable home."

She drew herself up, taking exception to the notion that only a two-parent home could give a child what he needed. She'd seen plenty of examples of a single parent being far better than a man and woman who didn't get along. "I can give them that," she said stiffly.

"Well, of course, you can. But boys especially need a man's influence. Where will they get that?"

Grace had no answer for that. He was right, too. Even though she didn't like admitting it, Jamie and Josh needed a male role model. Once again she was forced to consider whether she was being selfish in trying to keep them. Could she fight their feelings of abandonment any better alone than her mother had been able to fight hers?

"Just something to think about," Harlan Adams said mildly, then pushed himself up and reached for his cane. "Think I'll go outside and meet them now."

"I'll come with you," Grace offered.

"No need. Seems to me like you'd do better to spend a little time thinking about what I said."

"I will," she assured him. "I promise."

"A man can't ask for more than that." He stepped outside, then smiled at her. "It's been a pleasure, Grace. I look forward to seeing you again."

"The pleasure was all mine, Mr. Adams."

But after he had gone, she was left with the disquieting sense that despite his warm remarks, he didn't entirely approve of what she was planning. What she didn't understand was why that bothered her so. Could it be because she feared he might be right?

*  *  *

Michael looked up with surprise when he spotted Harlan Adams exiting the house and heading for the corral. Michael knew Harlan only from scattered casual meetings at Trish's wedding and later Dylan's. But he knew his reputation for taking charge and making things turn out the way he thought they ought to. No doubt it had been only a matter of time before he turned up here to check out what was going on, just as Justin had predicted he would.

"Mr. Adams, good to see you again," he said, crossing the yard to meet him.

"Thought I told you to call me Grandpa Harlan, like the rest of them. Said the same thing to that little gal inside, but she didn't pay a bit of attention to me either."

"Maybe we think it seems a bit disrespectful," Michael suggested.

"It's not if I say it isn't," Harlan said, then gazed around, his expression alight with curiosity. "Okay, then, where are they?"

"Jamie and Josh have gone off on their first real ride with Slade. They should be back any second. Would you care to have a seat over here by the corral? I can bring a chair from the barn."

"If you wouldn't mind, that would suit me fine. Bring two and sit a spell with me. It'll give us a chance to talk."

Uh-oh, Michael thought. "About?" he asked aloud.

The old man grinned. "This and that. It's not an inquisition, boy, so don't go getting your dander up already."

Michael let the comment pass, retrieved two chairs from the barn and took a seat next to Harlan.

"So, tell me," he said, casting a sly look at Michael. "What do you think of Grace's plan to take in those boys? Think she's taking on too much?"

"*She* doesn't think she is," Michael said.

"Now, that's not exactly what I asked you, is it?"

"No, I suppose not."

"Well, then?"

"I think Grace will give them a good home and the love they deserve."

"You gonna be around to be a role model for them?" he inquired pointedly. "Boys need the influence of a strong man."

"I suppose I'll see them from time to time," Michael replied cautiously, not especially crazy about the direction of the conversation. He knew all about Harlan Adams's penchant for matchmaking and his very large role in getting Trish and Hardy together. This was not the kind of pressure Michael needed, not right now when he and Grace were still finding their way.

"Seems to me like you need to do a little more than that, son," Harlan declared.

"It's not up to me," Michael insisted, not liking the glint in the old man's eyes one bit.

"Who's it up to, then? The court?" Harlan scoffed. "You think the court gives a hoot about the boys the way a father could? The judge isn't going to be there day in and day out. The judge isn't going to hug them or discipline them when they need it or see that they stay in school and get an education."

"Now wait just a damned minute," Michael protested. "How did we shift from maybe giving those two a male role model to me becoming their father?"

"You got other family obligations?" Harlan inquired tartly, as if that were the only issue to be considered.

"No, but—"

"No buts about it," the old man said, waving off Michael's attempted protest. "A man steps up to the plate in a situation like this. Does what's right. Looks to me as if that woman inside would be happy to take on the lot of you. Oh, she says she's got it all under control, that she doesn't need a lick of help, and maybe she doesn't, but people are meant to go through life sharing good times and bad with someone who'll understand."

Michael swallowed hard. This whole situation was spinning wildly out of control. "Grace and me?" he said as incredulously as if he hadn't known all along that this was where Harlan was heading, as if he hadn't considered the idea himself a time or two.

"Why on earth not? You blind, boy? The woman's beautiful. Smart, too. Had a little talk with her before I came looking for you. She's a keeper, the kind who'll stick by you. You're the one who called her over here at the first sign of trouble, am I right? And she came running."

"Oh, no, you don't," Michael protested, annoyed more by the pressure than by the concept of marriage to Grace. "I know about you and your matchmaking schemes. I am not in the market for a wife or a ready-made family. And when the time comes that I am, I will work out my own arrangements."

Harlan Adams just chuckled at that. "We'll see, son. We'll see."

Michael was still thinking about that long after the boys had returned, spent time with Harlan Adams, then gone inside to wash up for dinner. He had been thinking about spending more time with Grace, seeing where that led, but the rest? Marriage? A family? Was he ready to take that plunge?

And even if he suggested it, would Grace agree? He doubted it. She would probably howl with laughter all the way back to Houston. It would ruin the nice, steady courtship he'd had in mind.

Of course, a courtship implied a certain amount of intent, didn't it? Or was he just playing a game of semantics here? What the hell did he really want?

"Something on your mind, bro?" Tyler asked as he joined him, settling into the chair Harlan Adams had occupied earlier.

"Just thinking about something Harlan Adams said."

"Can I wager a guess about what it was?" He studied Michael intently. "He thinks you should marry Grace, adopt Josh and Jamie, and live happily ever after."

Michael stared at him. "How did you know that? I thought you were off riding with the boys. Were you eavesdropping instead?"

"No, but I've spent even more time around him than you have. The man dearly loves to meddle and he thinks everybody ought to be paired off and settled down. He's tried it on me a couple of times, but I always sneak out of town before his schemes can work."

He slanted a look toward Michael. "It's not such a bad idea, you know."

"What isn't?"

"You marrying Grace. You've been in love with her for who knows how long. Stupidity and pride got in the way last time, but there's no reason to let that happen again. I say go for it."

Michael grinned. "You always were her biggest fan."

"No, you were that. I was just an interested bystander who thought you were a damn fool for letting her get away."

"She'll turn me down," Michael said.

"How do you know?"

"I just do. She's not buying that I've changed."

Tyler chuckled. "You haven't."

"You're a help. Be sure to share that with Grace."

"Well, you haven't." He regarded Michael evenly. "You could, though, if it was for something you wanted badly enough. Do you want her that badly, Michael?"

"That's what I've been trying to figure out for the past couple of days."

"And?"

He felt a smile tugging at his lips. "I think I do."

"Now there's a declaration of passion guaranteed to make any woman's heart go pitter-patter."

"You know what I mean."

"No," he said evenly. "I don't. And if I'm not sure, Grace won't be either. Stop hedging your bets. It's time to go for broke or get out of the game."

Tyler was right. He had to make a clear choice, in or out. And he had to do it fast, before Grace created a loving, tight-knit little family that left him out in the cold.

## Chapter Thirteen

Michael had expected to feel calmer once Harlan Adams left for White Pines, but it wasn't turning out that way. In part that was his own fault. He was the one who'd invited Tyler over here. Now his brother refused to let the matter rest and was almost as interested in Michael's intentions toward Grace as the old man had been.

"Okay, bro," Tyler said as they sat on the deck while dusk settled in around them. "You dragged me over here because you anticipated some sort of problem. I assumed your concern was with Josh and Jamie. That problem hasn't materialized. After our conversation this afternoon and watching the two of you at dinner tonight, I have to wonder if you weren't just hoping I'd provide a buffer between you and your old feelings for Grace."

Irritated by the observation, Michael stared at his brother, cursing the fact that Tyler could read him like a book. "What the hell are you talking about?" he asked, feigning cranky innocence.

"You know exactly what I'm talking about. You've all but admitted it. You're still in love with her. You're scared to death to confess it to her, because then you'd have to risk being rejected for a second time."

"You're here because of Jamie and Josh, nothing else," Michael insisted.

"You did not need me just to get them out from underfoot for an afternoon. I'm sure Kelsey would have been happy to run over and pick them up, but you didn't even consider calling her, did you?"

"This could have gotten complicated," Michael said. "If Justin had gotten a notion to take those boys away today, I wanted backup to help me keep them here."

Tyler uttered a heavy sigh. "Okay, whatever you say, but I've got to tell you, if you let Grace get away again, I'm disowning you. Even a stubborn Delacourt should have enough sense to put pride aside and go for the gold."

"This isn't the blasted Romance Olympics," Michael muttered in disgust.

"You know what I mean."

"Yeah, I suppose I do."

Tyler stood up. "Good, then I can go back to Baton Rouge and face the music."

Michael's gaze shot to Tyler's face, but in the shadows he couldn't read his expression. "Ty, is ev-

erything okay? That's the second time you've al-
luded to a problem.''

"Nothing I can't handle," Tyler assured him
blithely. "You just worry about Grace."

"And Jamie and Josh," Michael reminded him.

Tyler chuckled. "Whatever. Let me know how
things turn out."

"You're sure you don't want to stay the night?"

"Nope. You're on your own. I've got places to go
and people to see."

Michael heard a worrisome note of dread under
his brother's light tone. "If there's anything I can do
to help," he said again.

"There isn't," Tyler assured him.

"Then I'll walk you out."

Out front he gave Tyler a hug. "Take care of yourself. Thanks for riding to the rescue."

"Not a problem. It gave me some breathing
space."

Again, there was that hint of trouble, but Michael
knew Tyler had already said all he intended to on
the subject, even though it was precious little. In fact,
it was rare that he even let this much leak out about
his personal life, which meant whatever it was had
to be weighing heavily on him.

For some time Michael had suspected Tyler was
involved with a woman he'd met in Louisiana while
working on a Delacourt Oil rig in the Gulf of Mexico, but his questions drew only the most cryptic,
uninformative responses. It was ironic really. Tyler
gave the impression of being the most open of the
brothers, yet he could keep his own counsel better
than any of them. One topic was absolutely off-limits

and that was his relationships. He withstood the teasing the rest of them dished out about his flirting in stoic silence.

After Tyler had gone, Michael returned to the deck. In no time the pressure that had begun building up in his chest earlier felt like it was about to explode. Options chased through his mind at a dizzying speed. He couldn't sort through them quickly enough, so he just counted his lucky stars that he had a few more days here with Grace, Jamie and Josh before they all went their separate ways. Grace and the boys together. Him alone.

The prospect of peace and quiet, of a return to routine, should have been heartening. Instead, the thought depressed him. He'd been going his own way for far too long. What had it really gotten him? His father relied on him, yes, but that would have happened anyway. Tyler had been right when he'd said that Michael was the only one in the family who really wanted an executive position. He would have won by default even if he'd devoted only half of his time and attention to the company.

Of course, that wasn't how he wanted to stay on top. He needed to prove himself, to be the best. For his own peace of mind, he needed to know he'd earned the right to head Delacourt Oil someday.

But hadn't he done that? Did he need to go on doing it forever, sacrificing everything else that really mattered?

Because he had no real answer to that question, he let his thoughts drift back to Grace and the boys. Those three would move on to Grace's apartment. He'd never been there, but he envisioned it as being cozy. The one they'd shared years ago had been, even though she'd furnished it on a shoestring with junk shop finds. She'd had a talent for mixing colors, for creating an atmosphere of warmth every bit as welcoming as what Trish had done with her home here.

He forced himself to face facts. If he didn't want to lose all three of them, he had to take action, do something. Anything. A grand gesture. Whatever.

For the next two days, though, Michael seemed plagued by indecision and inertia. Oddly enough, he had discovered that when the four of them were left alone, there was a certain comfort to be found in having two rambunctious, wise-ass boys underfoot and Grace's company on the front porch at the end of the day. He was even beginning to find a certain soothing delight in those blasted wildflowers.

He realized with a sense of astonishment that he hadn't called his office in several days. He didn't have to fill every empty minute of every quiet hour. He could just sit still, savor a morning cup of coffee on the deck, enjoy the view of Grace as she padded barefoot out to sit beside him, exposing shapely legs as she curled up on the lounge chair.

So, this was what it meant to relax, he concluded one lazy afternoon as he put aside a book and closed his eyes. It wasn't half-bad, especially with the sounds of boyish laughter echoing through the house and the occasional kiss from a woman who could send heat rocketing through him.

Despite the fact that everyone—himself included—seemed to expect something from him where Grace and those boys were concerned, he was surprisingly at ease. Maybe that was because Grace didn't seem to have any expectations at all. She just seemed glad to have company while she awaited further word on her petition to become a foster parent to Jamie and Josh.

He came to enjoy the mind-numbing monotony of the ranch routine, the laughter the four of them shared over cutthroat card games every night after dinner, the nonstop electricity that sparked between him and Grace.

In fact, he couldn't recall the last time he'd been as happy as he was right here, right now, sitting on the deck in the afternoon sun. Maybe this was what people meant when they talked about living in the moment, about not looking ahead or borrowing trouble.

"Michael?"

He opened his eyes and glanced up at Grace's worried expression. "What's wrong?" he asked, sitting up at once, heart thumping with sudden trepidation. He had the oddest sense that his contentment was about to be shattered. "Are Jamie and Josh okay?"

"They're fine, but I've been thinking."

"About?" he asked, when she didn't elaborate.

"Going back to Houston. I think it's time I took them there and got them settled in. I just spoke to the judge's office and got an okay. They'll notify me there when I need to be in court."

"I thought you took the whole week off. It's only Thursday," he protested, aware of a knot of tension forming in his stomach.

"I know, but they need time to adjust. I have to make some arrangements for them for next week, maybe a summer day camp. And I need to look for a bigger place. We can't all crowd into my apartment. There's a pull-out bed in my home office, but they won't be comfortable on that for long." She held up a sheet of paper. "I've been making a list. It's getting longer and longer. I have to get started or I'll panic."

Why had he foolishly thought that they would go on as they had been forever? Why had he counted on having more time? Obviously this living in the moment concept had a serious drawback. It left a person totally unprepared for the intrusion of reality.

"We can take the rental car and drive back," she went on, seemingly oblivious to his dismayed reaction.

"Don't be ridiculous," he said more tartly than he'd intended. At her surprised look, he forced himself to temper his tone. "When the time comes, you can take the corporate jet. I can have the pilot back over here in no time. Jamie and Josh will love it."

She grinned. "To tell you the truth, I was hoping you'd say that. They'll be thrilled. I imagine they've never flown before."

"You're sure you need to go now?" he asked, trying to buy himself more time to wrestle with the decisions he'd been avoiding.

"Yes. I know they're having a good time here, but I'm just beginning to realize how much needs to be done. I think we should go first thing tomorrow."

He studied her intently. "Second thoughts?"

"About taking them in? Never," she said fiercely.

"Then all the rest will fall into place," he said, offering a solace to her that he wished he could find for himself.

"What makes you so sure of that?"

"Because I know you. When there's a task at hand, you plunge in wholeheartedly. I've seen you accomplish miracles. You're an amazing woman, Grace, professionally and personally."

She regarded him with surprise. "Do you really mean that?"

"Of course. Why would you doubt it?"

"Professionally, at least, you and I almost never see eye-to-eye."

"I called you when I needed help, didn't I? Doesn't that prove how much I respect what you do, even if I'm often on the opposite side of a case from your client?"

"I suppose so," she said. "What about personally, though? I dumped you, remember?"

"I'm not likely to forget." He met her gaze. "I thought we were making progress on getting past that, too. A lot of progress, in fact."

Patches of color stained her cheeks. "Yes, I suppose we have."

"You aren't thinking that will end when we get back to Houston, are you?" He didn't like the heaviness in his chest as he awaited her reply.

"I guess that's up to you," she said. "You're the one with the nonstop schedule."

"If you can make time for Josh and Jamie in your schedule, then I can find time in mine for all of you," he declared emphatically.

"We'll see," she said, sounding blatantly skeptical.

Her tone was as good as a challenge. Michael resolved then and there that he would never give her a moment's doubt. He intended to see to it that he found a way to fit into her life...whether she wanted him there or not.

This wasn't just his second chance, as Tyler had reminded him. It was his last one.

The flight back to Houston the next morning was such an adventure for Josh and Jamie that Grace almost forgot that the moment they landed she and Michael would move back into their old familiar routines. Even though he'd promised to be there for her and the boys, she couldn't help wondering how long that would last once he set foot in the office. She knew what Bryce Delacourt was like. He was a demanding father and an even more demanding boss. He was the reason Michael had spent a lifetime trying to prove himself. He was chintzy with praise and generous with criticism, even though she knew he loved all of his sons. He couldn't seem to stop himself from doing the very things that drove most of them away.

At the airport as they left the plane, she spotted a limo waiting for them. Josh saw it, too.

"Wow, look at that car." Wide-eyed, he glanced up at Michael. "Do you think it belongs to somebody famous?"

"Not unless you think I'm famous," Michael said, grinning at him. "It's here for us."

"We don't want to take you out of your way,"

Grace said, not sure why she was resisting the offer. "We can take a taxi."

"The car's here," Michael countered. "And it's not out of my way."

"You don't even know where I live."

"Doesn't matter. I'm in no rush. Besides, I'd like to see where you live."

"Please, Grace," Josh begged. "We've never been in a fancy car like that."

His plea zeroed in on her real fear. With Michael offering them all of these luxuries—riding lessons, a company jet, a limo—would they be content with what she could give them? She made a comfortable living, but it didn't include this kind of perk.

Of course they would be content, she chided herself. They were the least materialistic kids she knew. While they had been grateful for the things they'd received, the opportunities they'd had the last few days, they weren't taking them for granted. What they really wanted was a loving home where they could be together, and she was giving them that. Nothing else mattered.

She lifted her gaze to meet Michael's speculative expression. "Thank you. We'd appreciate the lift."

When she had directed the driver to a high-rise condominium in the heart of downtown Houston, she saw Michael's eyebrows lift. It was definitely a far cry from the tiny apartment that they had once shared in Austin. That had been a temporary aberration, a blip in his life, a stepping-stone in hers.

This building was more in his league. She knew for a fact that he had once dated a socialite who lived on the penthouse floor. It had driven her crazy when she'd read about it in the paper, knowing that he was in the same building, making love with another woman. And that was during a time when she'd sworn to herself that she hated him. Obviously she'd been deluding herself for years. The past few days had proven that.

The boys were awestruck by the towering skyscraper, by the lobby and by the swift, silent elevator that whisked them upstairs.

"This is so cool," Josh said. "I could go up and down all day."

"No, you couldn't," Grace admonished. "It's not an amusement park ride."

Josh looked crestfallen. "I just meant it would be fun."

She ruffled his hair. "I know you did. I just want you to remember that there are lots of other people who need to use the elevator. It can't be going up and down just because you like to push the buttons."

"We won't even get on except when we have to," Jamie assured her, shooting a warning look at his brother as if he feared that one little mistake might ruin their chances of staying.

"I think that's enough talk about the elevator," Michael said. "Looks like we're here."

Grace led the way down the hall to her apartment, wondering what they would think of it. "Just remember," she said to the boys, "this will be temporary. We'll hunt for someplace with more room."

"Like a house?" Jamie said wistfully. "With a backyard?"

A house meant the suburbs, Grace thought, not entirely pleased by the prospect. That meant more driving than she was used to, more chances to get herself tangled up in traffic and thoroughly lost. It was also the way Jamie and Josh thought of home, the way she had once envisioned living.

"We'll look at houses," she agreed impulsively, as she unlocked the door to their current quarters.

When they walked inside, she wasn't sure which of them was more shocked. Jamie and Josh stared at everything, clearly stunned by the view and the very modern decor. She sensed that Michael's amazement was about something else entirely.

"It's not what I expected," he said candidly.

"Oh?"

"All this chrome and black and white," he said with a visible shudder. "It's not you."

"Maybe it is," she said defensively, rather than admitting that she had hated it on sight. She simply hadn't wanted to waste the time it would take to hire another decorator. She had given the woman free rein and refused to back down even when she'd been shaken by the way the woman apparently viewed her. She had consoled herself with the reminder that she was never here, anyway.

"I thought our place in Austin suited you better," he said, capturing her gaze. "I loved that apartment."

She swallowed hard. "You did?" The words were little more than a whisper.

"It made me feel good just walking through the door."

It had felt that way to her, too, but she had told herself it was because she was young and crazy in love. At that stage, she might even have liked *this* decor.

She glanced around at the sterile environment she rarely paid any attention to and reconsidered. Maybe not.

"Well, it is what it is," she said with a dismissive shrug. "I'm not here a lot."

"When do you plan on going house-hunting?" Michael asked.

"Tomorrow. Maybe the next day. I'll call a realtor."

"Let me know when you make an appointment."

"Why?"

"I'd like to come along."

If she hadn't had years to school herself never to show a reaction, her jaw might have dropped open. "You want to look at houses with us?"

"Why not? It'll be fun."

"Fine. If you're sure."

"I am," he said firmly. "Somebody has to make sure you don't do anything like this again."

She was certain that when the time came he would be tied up in meetings. Now that he was back in Houston, he wouldn't be able to resist sticking his head into the office, and that would be the end of his so-called vacation. It could be weeks before he surfaced again.

He stepped closer and tilted her chin up. "Everything okay?" he asked, lowering his voice so the boys wouldn't hear. Once they'd been granted permission, they had raced off to explore the rest of the apartment. "You look a little lost. Or maybe that's panic."

"I guess I am feeling a little overwhelmed," she admitted.

"Then why don't I come back around six, and we'll all go to dinner?"

"Won't you be tied up at the office?"

"I'm on vacation, remember?"

"I thought…"

"I know what you thought," he said, brushing a kiss across her lips. "But I'll be back, Grace. You guys discuss what you'd like to eat. I'll go along with anything."

The man who dined out at four-star restaurants was going to let two boys choose where they had dinner? Grace couldn't imagine it. But sure enough, a few hours later when they said they wanted Mexican fast-food, Michael didn't bat an eye. To her added amazement, he actually knew where the closest one was.

Crammed into a booth, the table littered with an assortment of tacos, burritos and nachos, she found herself wedged thigh-to-thigh beside him.

"If your friends could see you now," she teased.

"You think they never come here?" he said. "They have kids, too."

"They probably send them with the servants."

He peered at her intently. "When did you develop this reverse snobbery?"

Taken aback, she replayed what she'd said and sighed. "That is what it sounded like, isn't it? I'm sorry."

"No need. Are you having fun?"

"Actually I am," she admitted. Not that she could stop worrying about whether Michael thought he was slumming in some bizarre way, but beyond that she was enjoying being here with the three males who'd appeared so unexpectedly in her life.

"Good. Then you'll agree to buy some popcorn and rent a video when we leave here," he suggested. "Then after the boys are in bed, you and I can snuggle up on that monstrosity of a sofa."

"It's actually very comfortable," she said.

He winked. "I hope you're right, because I have big plans for that sofa."

"Michael!" she protested, casting a horrified look his way.

"Well, I do."

"Why are you doing this?"

"Doing what?"

"Acting like you're going to stick around?"

"Because I am."

"For how long? Till you go back to work next week?"

"No, darlin'. I thought I told you. I'm in this for the long haul."

Her pulse leaped, despite all the mental warnings that it was nothing more than a turn of phrase. Her gaze narrowed. "How long is that?"

"Five years. Twenty years. Who knows, maybe even fifty years."

"Five days is more like it."

He reached over with a napkin and dabbed at something at the corner of her mouth. Hot sauce probably. That would explain the burning sensation she felt at that exact spot. Surely, it wasn't because of his touch.

"Why don't we tackle this one day at a time," he suggested, "and see how long it adds up to be?"

She could do that. But could it possibly ever add up to enough to erase all these doubts that experience had taught her were totally justified?

## Chapter Fourteen

"Where have you been?" Bryce Delacourt demanded irritably when Michael poked his head into his father's office the next morning. Even though it was Saturday, he had known his father would be here. His only concession to the day of the week was leaving off his tie and jacket.

"I'm amazed you don't know," Michael retorted. "I thought your spies were better than that."

"Just answer the question."

"Your other children conspired against me."

His father's lips twitched with unexpected amusement. "Did they? That's twice now. They're cleverer than I've given them credit for being. Or you're not that great at learning from your mistakes."

Michael thought of the mistake he'd made in letting Grace get away years ago. He'd learned from that one, all right, but he wasn't ready to discuss it with his father. Instead he said, "Given how they've managed to slip out of your control, I would have thought you'd know better than anyone how inventive they can be."

"Don't remind me." His father pulled a thick pile of folders off the corner of his desk and held them out. "You need to go over these."

"No can do," Michael said, remembering his promise to Grace. He kept his hands clasped tightly behind his back to prevent himself from instinctively reaching for the work. "I'm still on vacation."

His father regarded him with surprise, then nodded. "Okay, take 'em home with you, then."

Michael grinned ruefully. "You seem to have the same problem with the concept of a vacation that I've had. Fortunately, I've reformed."

"Meaning?"

"Meaning no work, not this week anyway."

"But we've got to make a quick decision on some of these."

"Dad, you were making decisions for this company before I was born. I'm sure you can make a few more. If not, anything you've got there can surely keep until Monday."

His father's gaze narrowed. "You are my son, Michael, aren't you? The real Michael hasn't been kidnapped by aliens, has he?"

"Very funny. You've just proved what everyone else has been telling me. I spend too much time here. You count on me being a workaholic."

"Well, of course I do. Somebody's got to take over this place when I'm gone."

"And you'll probably be sitting right there at that desk when you drop over, won't you?" Michael said, realizing that he'd instinctively followed the example set by his father.

"A man can't ask for more than to die when he's doing something he loves," his father declared.

"What about being with the people he loves? Wouldn't that be better?"

His father studied him with a bemused expression. "What's gotten into you? You aren't thinking of ducking out on me, too, are you?"

"No," Michael assured him. "But I have discovered that there's a lot to be said for getting a little balance into my life."

"You spent too damned much time with your sister," his father grumbled. "You open your mouth and I can hear her talking. Can't imagine where she learned it, since your mother knows that hard work is what puts food on our table."

Michael uttered a harsh laugh. "Food? Dad, you could feed an entire nation with what you take home from here. Maybe we'd all have been a little richer if you spent time with us, instead."

His father sighed heavily. "Now I'm neglectful? That's your sister again. Blast her, isn't it enough that she bailed out on me? Does she need to start influencing you, too?"

"Actually Trish wasn't around all that much. She and Hardy took off to make sure I had lots of free time on my hands. Might have gone crazy if I hadn't had some unexpected company." He gestured toward the stack of bulging folders and grinned at his father. "Remind me to tell you about it one of these days when you don't have so much work piled up."

"Tell me now," his father commanded in a tone that normally would have brought Michael to a halt.

"No time. I'm going house-hunting." He stepped into the outer office and closed the door firmly behind him. Even through the thick mahogany paneling of the door and the top-of-the-line soundproofing, he could hear his father bellowing.

"House-hunting? You already have a house. Michael Delacourt, get back in here this instant and explain what the devil has happened to you."

Michael winked at his father's longtime secretary, who made it a habit to come in on Saturdays as well. She claimed it was for her own good. Otherwise, her desk was a disorganized mess on Mondays.

"You might want to steer clear of him for the next hour or two," he told her. "I seem to have thrown him off-stride."

She grinned. "It's about time. Whatever you're up to, Michael, have fun. You deserve it."

"I do, don't I?"

If his father had been startled by the changes in his attitude, Grace was positively stunned by his arrival promptly at ten.

"What are you doing here?" she demanded.

"The realtor's coming at ten, right? That's what you told me on the phone last night."

"Yes, but…"

"I told you I'd be here. Didn't you believe me?"

"Frankly, no. You also said you'd be stopping by the office on your way. I figured your father would have things for you to do."

"He did."

"And?"

"I told him to do them himself."

Her gaze widened. "You didn't."

He chuckled at her reaction. "He was even more shocked than you are, but he'll get over it." He leaned down and kissed her soundly. "Will you?"

She touched a finger to her lips. "I don't know."

"Where are Josh and Jamie? Surely you haven't locked them in their room for misbehaving already."

"No. They've discovered cable TV. Apparently there is an entire network devoted to cartoons. Thank goodness the realtor is due any minute. Otherwise, I doubt I'd pry them out of there before school starts in the fall."

Michael heard the squeals of laughter echoing down the hall. "Commandeered your office, too, I see. Until we watched that video last night had that TV ever actually been on before?"

"A couple of times when I was checking the news for reports on cases I had in court," she admitted.

Michael shook his head. "We're quite a pair, aren't we?" He smiled slowly. "Maybe we deserve each other."

Grace's gaze locked with his as if she weren't quite certain how seriously to take him.

Because there wasn't time to get into such a loaded topic right now with Jamie and Josh down the hall and a realtor on the way, he merely grinned. He was feeling good today, no doubt about it.

He winked at her. "Something to think about, isn't it?"

\* \* \*

Grace had been off-kilter ever since Michael had actually shown up on time. Forget on time. The fact that he'd shown up at all had been shocking. She didn't know what to make of his attitude or his innuendoes. If the man was toying with her, hinting at a future he had no intention of sharing with her, she'd have to strangle him. No doubt about it.

She glanced into the kitchen of the house the realtor was currently showing them and heard Michael cross-examining her about the age of the appliances, the taxes, the utility bills and a zillion other details she hadn't even thought about discussing. She would have, though. Before she made an offer on a house, she surely would have remembered to ask those same questions, rather than daydreaming about bright color schemes and comfortable sofas.

The only problem was she had hated this house on sight. It was huge and pretentious. Even though the boys obviously loved the big backyard and the pool, she didn't think she could bring herself to live in a showplace like this. It reminded her too much of the Delacourt mansion.

"Grace?" Michael was looking at her curiously. "You okay?"

"Fine."

"What do you think?"

"I hate it," she said candidly, grateful that the realtor wasn't nearby to hear. Curious about his reaction to a place that so closely resembled his home, she asked, "How about you?"

"Hate it," he agreed. "Maybe we'd better tell her she's on the wrong track or we'll waste an entire day looking at houses that are pumped up versions of a Southern plantation.''

She chuckled at the description. ''That's exactly what it is, isn't it? You talk to her. If I try, I'm liable to laugh out loud. She might consider that an insult to her taste. To tell you the truth, I doubt she would have shown me this place if she hadn't recognized your name. She probably figures we're trying to outdo your family.''

''Heaven forbid,'' Michael said with a shudder. ''Okay, I'll talk to her. You try to keep the boys out of the pool. They're itching to dive in. Any second now one of them is going to give the other a shove, then claim it was an accident.''

Grace glanced through the French doors that opened onto the pool deck and saw Josh and Jamie inching ever closer to the side. She bolted for the door.

''Okay, you two, back inside.''

''Grace, this is so cool,'' Josh said. ''Are you gonna buy it?''

''No.''

''Aw, how come?'' Josh asked. ''It would be really cool having our very own pool.''

Jamie fought to cover his disappointment with disdain for his brother. ''Probably 'cause it's too expensive, dummy.''

''It's not too expensive,'' Grace said. ''It's just way too fancy.''

''We wouldn't mess things up,'' Josh promised, regarding her hopefully.

''I'm sure you would try very hard not to,'' she

agreed. "I'm not worried about that. I just want someplace that'll be more comfortable."

"You mean like with chairs and stuff?" Jamie asked. "It'd have furniture, Grace. Maybe you'd like it better then."

She ruffled his hair. "I doubt that. Don't look so disappointed. This is only the first house we've seen. The perfect house is out there."

Unfortunately, after two more hours of looking and a break for lunch, they had still seen nothing that fit her idea of a real home.

Michael seemed to agree with her. Once he'd paid for lunch and they were outside waiting for valet parking to return their cars, he turned to the real estate agent. "Thanks for all your help this morning, Mrs. Norton. I think we need some time to fine-tune our needs."

Grace stood up a little straighter. *Our needs?* What the devil did he mean by that? This was her house. She'd let him speak for her earlier, but somehow he'd apparently gotten it into his head that he had a say in what she ultimately chose.

"Michael, could I speak to you for a second?" she said urgently, drawing him aside as the realtor gave him a speculative look. "What are you doing? It's bad enough that she defers to you on every little detail. She needs to know that I'm the customer. There is no *us.*"

"Do you want to look at more houses with her?"

"No, but—"

"Then let me shake her."

"I should be the one to do that."

He shrugged, regarding her with amusement. "Then, by all means, do it."

Grace returned to Mrs. Norton. "Thank you so much for your help this morning," she said graciously.

"You're entirely welcome. Shall we take a look at just one more house. I think I've narrowed down the possibilities, based on your earlier reactions. This could be the one."

Grace doubted it, but the woman was so eager, how could she possibly refuse. "One more," she agreed with a barely contained sigh. She had to try very hard to ignore Michael's *I-told-you-so* look.

Naturally the last house was no better than any of the others. In fact, it could have been a cookie-cutter copy of the first house, except for the color scheme which ran toward burgundy and forest green. Grace actually liked those colors, but not when they were done in heavy velvet and damask fabrics that blocked out every bit of sunlight. It took everything in her to hide her horrified reaction.

This time when she dismissed the realtor, she had no trouble at all doing it forcefully.

As she, Michael and the boys climbed back into the car, Josh declared, "That place gave me the creeps. It looked like ghosts could live there."

Jamie poked his brother in the ribs. "It's not polite to say stuff like that."

"It is in this case," Michael said. "I expected to find a vampire's coffin in one of the bedrooms."

Grace chuckled. All three males stared at her, then burst into laughter.

"It was so awful," she said, choking out the words

between giggles. Then the enormity of what lay ahead of her in finding a dream house sank in. Her laughter died as quickly as it had begun.

"Let's stop by my place," Michael suggested, his expression enigmatic, though it was evident to her that he had guessed she was verging on hysteria. "The boys can go for a swim and you and I can have a tall glass of something cold to drink while we rethink our strategy."

"You're going to keep helping us look?" she asked, surprised and relieved that this wasn't going to be the only day he could dedicate to house-hunting.

"Absolutely. I'm terrified you'll get so worn out that last place will start to look good to you."

"Not a chance of that," she said.

"All the same, I think I'll stick around."

A few minutes later he turned onto a side street in a quiet, older neighborhood where the houses were large, but looked as if real people lived in them. Lawns were mowed, not manicured, and were littered with bicycles and other evidence that there were children on the block.

Grace turned to him in surprise. "You live near here?"

"Just up the street," he confirmed.

"But it's so..." Words failed her.

"Normal?" he suggested. "That's what I wanted. My secretary helped me find it. She lives about a mile from here."

"Are you sure you didn't pick it just so she'd be conveniently located to handle any middle-of-the-night brainstorms you might have?" Grace teased.

"Her husband is an ex-Oiler linebacker. He doesn't permit middle-of-the-night brainstorms." He leveled a look at her. "I bought this place because it reminded me of someplace I used to feel at home."

Could he be talking about their apartment? Grace wondered. That tiny place in what could only be described as a transitional neighborhood wasn't even close to being in the same league as this. Surely she was mistaken about what he meant.

When he turned into a tree-lined driveway, Grace noticed that his house was on a larger lot than most and set well back from the road. A hedge afforded it some privacy. Beyond that, the house itself was much like its neighbors, built of light-colored brick, trimmed in white, with an attached two-car garage on the side. Shrubs and flowers added splashes of color.

"It's lovely," Grace said, something deep inside responding to its welcoming appearance and to the fact that a wealthy, powerful man like Michael had chosen a down-to-earth home like this.

When they walked through the front door, she had to keep herself from gasping in surprise. It was open and airy and filled with the same kind of cozy touches that had made Trish's house so appealing. The same kind he had told her he'd loved about their apartment.

"I had it gutted down here to create a more open feeling. Trish helped me out with the decorating," he said, his gaze intense, maybe even a little worried. "Do you like it?"

"Like it? I love it. The colors, all those windows looking out on the backyard, the trees and flowers.

It must feel as if you're living in a garden, just like it does at Trish's.''

He regarded her with surprise. ''I never thought of it that way, but I suppose it does,'' Michael said. ''I guess I tried to create what we had once along with what she had in Los Piños without even realizing it.''

Josh and Jamie had their noses pressed to the glass doors, eyeing the inviting, crystal blue pool.

''Can we really swim while we're here?'' Josh asked.

''Sure. There are extra suits in that room off the kitchen. There should be a couple that fit. Don't go in the water, though, until Grace and I get out there.''

''How long will that be?'' Josh asked impatiently.

''Not long,'' Grace assured him.

''As soon as I show her the rest of the house,'' Michael said, then held out his hand. ''Come see the upstairs.''

Like the downstairs, each room brought the outdoors in with huge windows and complementary bedspreads in the dark greens and splashy florals of the gardens outside. She counted three bedrooms before he led her to the master suite.

''Best for last,'' he said, stepping aside to let her walk in.

It was, too. She could imagine him in this room with its crisp, clean fabrics and soft sage color. The dresser was littered with framed family photos. Gold cufflinks were tossed carelessly aside next to scattered change.

Then there was the bed. Oh, my, she thought as her eyes widened and her pulse kicked up. It was a huge, thoroughly decadent bed with a thick, puffy comforter and piles of pillows. She could imagine making love in that bed, then snuggling together under those covers for warmth as a chilly breeze stole in from the open doors that led onto a small balcony overlooking the backyard and the forested property beyond.

"What do you think?" Michael asked.

Grace's mouth was dry. Words wouldn't seem to form.

He grinned. "Tempting isn't it?" he asked, stepping up behind her and circling her waist. He linked his fingers loosely in front of her and rested his chin on top of her head. She could feel his breath fanning across her cheek.

"More than you know," she said honestly.

"Gracie?"

He never called her that except when they were alone and intimate. She trembled at the memories of him whispering it at the height of passion.

"Move in here."

She broke free of his embrace to stare. "Here?"

"Why not? You love it. The boys will, too."

"I can't," she said at once. "We can't. The court would have a cow about me bringing those two boys to live with you."

He had the audacity to chuckle at her indignation. "You mean if we were living here in sin, so to speak."

"Well, of course. And it's nothing to joke about, Michael."

"I'm not joking, Gracie. And I'm not suggesting we set up some sort of informal living arrangement. I want you to marry me. I want us to be a family.

This house was made for lots of kids. It was made for us. We can be happy here.''

Listening to him, Grace knew the real meaning of temptation. This house. Michael. It was all she'd ever dreamed of, but he'd neglected to mention one thing. He hadn't said anything at all about love. They would need a lot of it if they were going to make it, a lot of it as they learned the art of compromise.

The old Michael had had absolutely no experience with the concept of compromise. She had no reason to believe he'd changed.

''I can't marry you,'' she said sadly. ''I want to, more than you'll ever know, but I can't.''

He stiffened at her refusal and his eyes darkened with hurt. ''Why is that? I thought we'd made progress the last few days.''

''We have,'' she agreed. ''But it hasn't even been a week, Michael, and old habits die hard.''

''Which old habit are we talking about? You hating me for letting you down?''

She winced at the direct hit. She wanted to believe the accusation was unfair, but maybe it wasn't. Maybe she hadn't entirely forgiven him for the past. Maybe she needed a whole lot more than a few days worth of evidence before she believed he'd really changed.

''No, you caring about anything more than your job,'' she said quietly.

''I see.''

''Maybe I should get the boys and go,'' she said, feeling as if something inside had shattered. Her heart, maybe.

"No, stay. Let them have their swim. I'm sure you and I can maintain a polite facade for their sake."

"Dammit, Michael, I don't want to maintain any kind of a facade. This is about facing reality. I won't set those two up for more disappointments. I can't."

He shook his head, regarding her with something that might have been pity. "It isn't about disappointing them, Grace. It's about disappointing you. You're scared to take a chance. The worst part is that on one level I can't really blame you for that. I just don't know how to prove to you that I will never let you down again."

And that, she thought, was the saddest thing of all, because she didn't know how he could, either.

## Chapter Fifteen

Michael had every intention of fighting for Grace, of doing whatever it took to convince her that they should be a family. He knew she loved him, knew that they could make it work, but he had to find a way to prove it to her. Unfortunately, he didn't have a clue what that proof might be.

And then, just before dawn on Monday morning, his phone rang, waking him from a sound sleep. At first he couldn't grasp what his mother was saying.

"Mother, slow down. You're not making any sense."

"It's your father, Michael. He got out of bed a little while ago and went to the kitchen to make coffee." She choked back a sob. "That's where I found him, in the kitchen, on the floor."

Michael felt his heart slam against his ribs. "Is he okay? What happened?"

"The paramedics say he's had a heart attack. I don't know how serious it is, but he hasn't come to. That can't be good, Michael. They've taken him to the hospital. Can you call the others and meet me there?"

"I'm on my way," Michael said at once. "Mother, get a neighbor to drive you, okay? Promise me. Don't drive while you're this upset."

"Pauline is here. She'll take me."

Pauline was the housekeeper who had been with them for the past ten years. She was as close as family and she was a rock in a crisis. She would take good care of his mother.

Michael yanked on the first clothes he could grab, then raced to his car. He spent the drive to the hospital making calls on his cell phone. He caught up with Dylan, who'd miraculously returned home to Los Piños, probably five seconds after Michael's departure. Dylan promised to call Trish.

"We'll be over there as fast as we can get there. Call me if you have any news in the meantime."

"I will."

"He's going to be okay, Michael. Dad's tough. He'll outlive us all."

"I pray you're right," Michael said. He had this terrible, gut-deep fear that his behavior on Saturday had been the blow that caused this. Had his father felt Michael slipping away as the others had done? Was he convinced that all his years of hard work to build an empire for his family had been wasted? If so, that would have created unbearable stress for a man like Bryce Delacourt.

Because he couldn't bear to think about that, he concentrated on trying to track down Jeb on his honeymoon. When he finally reached him, Jeb was ready to fly home immediately.

"Wait," Michael advised. "I'll call you back as soon as I get to the hospital. Let's see where we are, before you cut your honeymoon short."

"I need to be there," Jeb protested.

"You won't get here in the next fifteen minutes. Sit tight for that long, at least. Then you can decide."

"Call me the minute you know anything."

"I promise."

That left Tyler, but try as he might, Michael couldn't locate his brother anywhere, not at his apartment in Houston, not at work on the oil rig.

"I'll track him down," the supervisor of operations at the rig said.

"Do you even know where to look?"

"He spends a lot of time in Baton Rouge. If he's there, one of the men will locate him."

"Thanks," Michael said, hanging up just as he turned into the hospital parking lot, tires squealing.

Minutes later, he found his mother in the emergency room waiting area, looking as unkempt as he'd ever seen her in public. It was testament to her panic that she hadn't even combed her hair or changed out of her bathrobe. She was crying silently as Pauline patted her hand and murmured reassurances. The housekeeper spotted him first and stood up to give him a fierce hug.

"It's good you're here, Michael. She's going to make herself sick with worrying."

"Has there been any word yet?"

"Nothing," Pauline said.

He gave his mother a quick kiss, then said to the housekeeper, "Stay with her. I'll see what I can find out."

It turned out to be easier said than done to get a straight answer. Either no one he approached knew anything or they were too busy to stop and explain what was happening.

"Please, Mr. Delacourt, the doctor will be out to talk to you as soon as he has a minute," a nurse told him at the entrance to what was apparently his father's treatment cubicle. "You can't come in here. Let the doctor do his job."

He glanced past her. All he could see amid the cluster of doctors and nurses and machines was a glimpse of ashen skin. "Is he going to make it?"

"This team is the best. They'll give him every chance humanly possible. The rest will be up to God. Maybe you could spend some of this waiting time praying to Him."

Michael knew the suggestion was well-meant, but he'd been praying all the way over here. He wanted answers now. He felt a reassuring touch on his shoulder and turned to find Grace regarding him with a concerned expression.

"Michael, let them work."

Shock at finding her here was rapidly replaced by relief. He desperately needed her right now, needed to hold onto something real and positive. "How did you hear about this?"

"It was on the radio. I was on my way to the courthouse when I heard it. I knew you'd be here and that you'd be causing trouble."

He managed an exhausted grin. "You know me, I hate anything I can't control."

"He'll be okay," she said. "Believe that."

"If only it were that simple."

"I spoke to your mother. She's holding up okay. As soon as we get back there to be with her, Pauline said she was going to go home and get some clothes for her. Come on, let's go keep her company. The sooner she gets to freshen up a bit, the better she'll feel."

She turned, but when Michael didn't follow at once, she glanced back. "What?"

"You have no idea how glad I am that you're here." He shook his head, hoping to clear it of this fog of disbelief that made everything that had happened this morning seem surreal. "I'm scared, Grace. The only other time I've been this scared was when you walked out on me."

She opened her mouth to respond, but no words came out. Instead, she simply took his hand and squeezed it. The gesture, her presence, provided more comfort than he had any right to expect.

As they waited for what seemed to be an eternity, Grace encouraged his mother to talk, then told her about Josh and Jamie, anything to keep her distracted. Finally, at nine-thirty, a tall man in green scrubs came into the waiting area looking for them. Michael tried to read his expression, but for once his ability to gauge moods failed him.

The doctor took a seat beside Michael's mother.

"I won't lie to you," he said. "It was touch and go for a while in there, but we have your husband stabilized for now. I've got an operating room waiting. He needs a triple bypass and he needs it now. I'd like to wait, but, frankly, I don't think that's an option."

"Without it, he'll die?" his mother asked in a hushed whisper.

"Let's just say I don't like the odds if we wait," the doctor said. "I've been trying to get him to come in for a test for months now, but he wouldn't take the time."

So this wasn't as unexpected as Michael had thought. His father had seen a cardiologist, then ignored his advice. That was typical of him.

"Has he been conscious at all?" his mother asked.

"He's been in and out. Now he's sedated."

His mother looked at him. "Michael, what do you think?"

"There's no choice, Mother. We have to let him perform the surgery. We have to give Dad that chance." He leveled a look straight at the doctor. "Could he die anyway?"

"Yes," the doctor said bluntly. "But the odds of him pulling through go up considerably if he makes it through the operation, makes some lifestyle changes, eats better, gets rid of some of the stress in his life."

Michael nodded. "We'll see to it, doctor. You keep him alive through the surgery and we'll see to the rest."

Tyler's litany of warnings came back to haunt him. Was this the future he faced if he didn't make those same changes? One glance at Grace proved she was thinking the same thing. She didn't need to say a word for him to get the message loud and clear.

The next few hours passed in a complete haze. Dylan and Trish arrived. Michael spoke to Jeb and filled him in. This time Jeb wouldn't be dissuaded from coming home.

"Brianna agrees. We belong there. We've already made reservations. We'll be there tonight. Is everyone else accounted for?"

"Everyone except Tyler," Michael said. "I can't find him. He's not answering his cell phone. His boss is trying to track him down in Baton Rouge."

"Keep trying. He'll never forgive himself if something happens to Dad and he's not there."

"I know."

"You okay, Michael?"

He glanced at Grace, who gave him a quick, reassuring smile. "Yeah, I'm hanging in there, thanks to a little help from an old friend."

"Care to explain that one?"

"You'll see when you get here."

When he'd tucked the cell phone back in his pocket, Grace left the conversation she was having with Trish and his mother to come to him.

"How about some coffee? Something to eat?"

"Nothing." He smacked his fist against the wall. "Damn, I hate this waiting."

"I know."

"Where are Jamie and Josh?"

"I made arrangements for a neighbor to keep them while I was at work today."

"Work?" He stared at her blankly, then shook

himself. "Of course, it's Monday, isn't it? Shouldn't you be there?"

"It was more important for me to be here."

She said it matter-of-factly, but Michael heard something else in her voice. She was sending yet another message about her priorities and how she had always put the people in her life first. Unlike him.

As if she sensed his troubled thoughts, she gave his hand another squeeze. "It's okay, Michael. I will have to go soon, though. I promised her I'd pick them up by four."

Michael glanced at his watch, stunned to see that it was after three. "What the hell is taking so long?"

"This isn't something you want them to rush," she reminded him quietly.

"No, no, of course not."

No sooner had he spoken than the doctor came through the swinging doors. Michael introduced him to Dylan and Trish, then asked, "Well, how did it go?"

"He came through the surgery like the stubborn old man he is. He's in recovery now. We'll move him to Cardiac Intensive Care later. He'll be there a few days."

"Then?"

"If all goes well, he'll go into a regular room and be home by the weekend, chomping at the bit to go back to work. I'd suggest you prevent that if humanly possible," he said with a slight grin.

"I'll see that he doesn't," Michael said grimly.

"No, I will," his mother said forcefully. "He will not set foot in the office until I say it's okay. I don't care if that blasted company goes bankrupt in the meantime.''

All of them stared at her in shock.

''Well, I don't. It's robbed me of too many years with my husband as it is. I won't let it steal him from me forever. And that's final.''

Dylan turned slowly to Michael. ''You going to be able to take up the slack?''

''Of course,'' he said firmly, but even as he spoke he saw Grace's expression of dismay. She whirled around and took off down the hall before he could break away to catch her.

Couldn't she see that he had no choice, that this was an emergency? How could he make her understand that this didn't change his promise to her, that he still intended to do everything in his power to spend time with her and Josh and Jamie?

All the way home Grace told herself she was being unreasonable. Of course Michael had to step in and help out while his father recuperated. But she knew in her heart that this was no temporary measure. Even if Bryce Delacourt recovered fully, his wife would see to it that he didn't go back to working at the same pace he'd set for himself before. She had heard that determination in Mrs. Delacourt's voice. That left the day-to-day operation of the company to Michael. He would immerse himself in it, because that was his nature and because he saw it as his duty.

It didn't help that Josh and Jamie greeted her with a hundred questions about Michael's whereabouts.

''I want to tell him about all the neat stuff we did today,'' Josh said.

"He can't come over tonight," Grace told them, knowing that unless she put an end to their expectations now, they would go on being disappointed. "His father's in the hospital."

"Is he gonna die?" Jamie asked, looking worried.

"It looks as if he'll make a full recovery," Grace said. "But this means that Michael is going to be very, very busy for quite a while with the family business. I don't think we'll see too much of him."

Josh looked ready to cry, but Jamie just regarded her stoically. "I figured he wouldn't stick around. Who cares? We don't need him."

Grace gathered both boys close and gave them a fierce hug. The problem was they did need him. All of them did. And maybe she needed Michael most of all.

Everyone else had gone home to get some much-needed sleep, but Michael remained in the waiting area outside of the intensive care unit, slouched down in an uncomfortable chair, drinking coffee the strength of battery acid.

That was where Tyler found him at midnight.

"How is he?" he demanded, his gaze shifting from Michael to the doors of the cardiac unit.

"Where the hell have you been?"

"It doesn't matter," Tyler said, raking his hand through his hair. "How is he?"

"He'll make it."

Tyler sank down on a plastic chair. "Thank God. I was scared to death I wouldn't get here in time."

"Even Jeb and Brianna beat you here," Michael said, not cutting his brother any slack.

"The point is, I came the minute I heard."

"Tyler, where were you? It's not like you to just up and disappear."

"I was living my life," Tyler snapped back. "It's something you should consider." Before Michael could utter a sharp retort, he added, "I suppose you'll bury yourself in work again to take up the slack while Dad's out."

"Of course I will. You might consider coming back for a while, too."

"Not a chance. And if you have an ounce of sense in your head, you won't do it either."

"Dammit, somebody in this family has to be responsible," Michael said.

"And it always has to be you."

"In this instance, yes."

"How does Grace feel about that?"

Michael winced as he thought of the expression on her face when she'd run out earlier.

"Not jazzed about it, is she?" Tyler asked.

"We haven't discussed it."

"But she knows what you intend to do?"

"Yes."

Tyler shook his head. "Look, I know I'm the jokester, the playboy, whatever, but listen to me just this once. Haven't you learned anything from what happened today? Life is short. You've got a woman who's crazy about you, a couple of kids who desperately need a dad. Weigh that against one more merger, one more high-powered negotiation. I know which one Mother would tell you to choose."

Michael knew, too. Her vehement comments earlier had pretty much destroyed any illusion that she'd been content with the way his father had neglected their marriage in favor of the business.

"You know something else?" Tyler said. "I'll bet if you ask Dad the same question right now, he might surprise you with his answer."

Michael wasn't so sure about that. Bryce Delacourt was stubborn, but Michael hoped not to be known for quite the same level of muleheadedness. He stood up.

"Where are you going?" Tyler asked, a faint grin tugging at the corners of his mouth. "Or need I ask?"

"I just hope she'll let me in."

"She might not," Tyler agreed. "But if she does, I hope you'll have sense enough to go in there, barricade the door and keep asking her to marry you until she says yes."

Michael laughed. "I might have to do just that."

In the end, getting in was even harder than he'd expected. Josh answered the phone when Michael called from the lobby.

"What are you doing up?" he asked.

"Grace is crying," Josh announced. "And it's your fault."

Grace crying? "I'm coming up," he said. "Can you hit the button to buzz me in?"

"I don't know how."

"Get Jamie."

"He's real mad at you."

"Get him anyway."

The phone clattered on the table as Josh went looking for his brother. A minute later, Jamie answered sleepily.

"What do you want?"

"I want to come up and talk to Grace."

"Well, she don't want to see you. None of us do."

"I do," Josh protested.

"Look, Jamie, it's the middle of the night. Just buzz me in."

"Why do you want to see Grace?"

He was explaining himself to a thirteen-year-old, Michael thought wearily. It was worse than going to a disapproving father to ask for a daughter's hand in marriage.

"I need to explain some things to her."

"What things?"

Michael thought he detected a faint click on the line. He suspected Grace had picked up an extension to see what was going on in the middle of the night.

"That I love her, for starters," he said, praying that he was right about her being on the line. "That I want to marry her and be a father to you guys. And that I am not going to wind up following in my father's footsteps, not into a hospital room, anyway."

There was a buzz on the line. Michael grabbed the door to the lobby and yanked it open. The elevator seemed to take forever, but when it opened upstairs, Grace was standing in the hallway, clutching her robe around her.

"You have a lot of nerve," she said as he came toward her. "It's the middle of the night, for one thing. For another, you woke up the boys. For another, you told them things you've never said to me."

He chuckled. "How do you know that unless you were listening?"

"You knew I was on the line?"

"Of course."

"So you said all of that for my benefit?"

"Yes."

She searched his face. "I want to believe you."

"You can, darlin'. I've learned a lot of lessons today. At the top of the list is the fact that I don't want to go through life without you and I want our life together to be a very long one."

"The company's going to need someone to run it the next few months."

"The company has a very good executive team. It's about time we gave them more to do."

"Do you honestly mean that?"

He brushed a wisp of hair away from her cheek. "I honestly do." He rubbed the pad of his thumb across her lower lip and felt her tremble. "So, Grace Foster, are you going to marry me and keep me from turning into a workaholic like my father?"

"You're the only one who can do that, buster," she said forcefully, then grinned. "But I guess I'll have to marry you just to make sure you have a really good incentive."

He lowered his head and claimed her mouth. When he finally lifted his head again, he murmured, "That's the best incentive I can think of. I'm still going to want your kisses on my hundredth birthday."

"You'd better."

Michael glanced toward Grace's apartment and spotted two towheaded kids trying not to be seen as they blatantly eavesdropped. He gave a nod in their direction for Grace's benefit, then said, "Think we should have kids right away?"

"As far as I'm concerned, we already do," she said.

"You mean Josh and Jamie?" he inquired innocently.

"Those are the ones. We're a package deal, Delacourt."

"You drive a tough bargain, Ms. Foster. But then you always did."

"Is he saying yes?" Josh whispered.

"Not in plain English," Jamie grumbled.

"Yes," Michael said loudly.

"Oh, wow," Josh breathed, racing into the hall and catching him around the legs in a hug.

Jamie sauntered out more slowly.

"Does this sound okay to you?" Michael asked. "All of us together, a real family?"

"Are you gonna, like, adopt us?"

Michael met Grace's gaze, then nodded. "If we can and only if you both agree."

"Say yes," Josh pleaded. "Come on, Jamie. We'll be together forever and ever. All of us."

Jamie finally released a pent-up sigh and a smile slowly spread from ear to ear. "Yes."

"I guess that makes it official," Michael said, just before he snatched the chance to steal one more long, satisfying kiss.

"Oh, yuck, more mushy stuff," Josh and Jamie declared in unison.

"The mushy stuff is the only thing in life that really counts," Michael told them. "You'll see."

"Hopefully," Grace said. "It certainly took you long enough to catch on."

"But I was worth waiting for, wasn't I?"

She winked at him. "That remains to be seen."

## Epilogue

"I ain't never been on a honeymoon before," Josh said as Michael and Grace studied the travel brochures spread out on the dining room table at Michael's house.

"And you're not going on this one," Michael said.

"How come?"

"'Cause it's all about mushy stuff," Jamie said wisely. "They don't want little kids around."

"Where are we gonna stay?"

"With Grandpa Bryce," Michael said.

Grace regarded him worriedly. "I'm not so sure that's such a good idea. He's still recuperating."

"If mother has her way, he'll be recuperating for another year at least, but even she admits he's going stir-crazy. These two ought to keep him occupied and safely at home where she can keep an eye on all of them.''

''I like staying with Grandpa Bryce,'' Josh said. ''He lets us play with his computer.''

Michael looked stunned. ''He does?''

''Uh-huh. Last time, he taught us how to figure out profit and loss figures for the year.''

Grace groaned. ''The man never gives up. He's already working on the next generation and these two aren't even related to him.''

''Not yet,'' Michael said. ''But they're going to be. The court date is next month.'' He glanced around. ''Any second thoughts? Last chance to back out of this adoption business.''

''Not me,'' Josh said fervently.

''Me, either,'' Grace said.

Michael turned his gaze to the silent thirteen-year-old. ''Jamie?''

''Nah. I think it might be pretty cool to finally have a mom who's really around and a dad.''

''Not half as cool as I think it's going to be to have two sons to follow in my footsteps,'' Michael said.

Grace frowned at the comment. ''I can still call this wedding off,'' she said. ''It doesn't have to happen.''

Three male voices protested in unison.

''Okay, then, no more talk about anybody following in anybody's footsteps. Understood?''

''Yes ma'am,'' they all said dutifully, Michael included.

Grace grinned. It was very rewarding that only a few days away from her wedding, they finally knew who was in charge. She wasn't about to delude herself, though. It was three-against-one, if push ever came to shove.

Which was why when she and Michael were finally in the honeymoon suite overlooking the ocean in Hawaii, she slipped out of her negligee and lured him straight into bed, ignoring the food and champagne he'd ordered.

"You seem to be in some sort of a hurry, Mrs. Delacourt. Why is that?"

"I want to make love with you. Surely you knew that was what we'd be doing on our honeymoon. You know, the mushy stuff."

"Oh, really? I'd hoped to squeeze in a couple of business meetings."

She barely resisted the urge to smack him. "Not in this lifetime," she assured him as she began working on the buttons of his shirt.

"I detect the fact that you have an agenda here. Care to fill me in?"

"I want a baby, Michael."

"We're just about to adopt two hellions. Isn't that enough family for now?"

Grace shook her head. "Nope. I think we need a couple of little girls. Did I ever mention that twins run in my family? On my mother's side. Her mother was a twin. So was my great-great-great-grandmother. It seems to skip every generation or two. I figure we're about due."

His head snapped up at that. "Twins?"

"Just think about it," she murmured, tugging his belt loose. "Won't it be wonderful?"

Michael looked dazed. "Wonderful," he said finally.

Grace shimmied his pants down his legs, then gave him a gentle nudge that had him tumbling backwards onto the bed. She climbed on top of him.

"Have I mentioned that you're going to be a terrific family man, Mr. Delacourt?"

He gave her a wicked grin, then flipped her onto her back. "But first I have to prove what an outstanding husband I can be," he said softly, his mouth moving over her.

Grace felt the familiar rise of heat, the familiar buildup of tension as his wildly clever fingers teased and taunted until her body trembled.

"Michael, please," she murmured when it seemed she was about to be swept away on a tide of delicious sensations.

"Please what?"

"Please show me what an outstanding husband you're going to be," she murmured, reaching for him, sliding her hand over the length of his arousal.

He moaned at her touch, then hesitated above her before slowly sliding deep inside, filling her up, making her whole. The rhythm he set was sweet torment, slow, then fast, then slow again until every nerve ending was on fire, every muscle tense as she strained toward an elusive peak.

And, then, when she was almost there, he stole another one of those devastating kisses, the ones that melted her inside. This time it was just what she needed to hurtle over the edge into spasms of pure ecstasy.

Exhausted, she curled against him. "That was—"

"Outstanding," he suggested, his hand on her breast, already starting something again.

"Better than outstanding," she said and placed one hand on her tummy. "We've made babies, Michael. I just know we have."

He regarded her with tolerant amusement. "Darlin', if we haven't, it will certainly be my pleasure to go on trying."

"I love you, Mr. Delacourt."

"I love you," he whispered solemnly, then added, "More than anything."

Hearing the words meant a lot, but deep in her heart, Grace had already known it was true. She intended to spend the rest of her life making sure that never changed.

\* \* \* \* \*

*Watch what happens when
a woman bent on revenge
turns Tyler's life into chaos in*

**THE DELACOURT SCANDAL,**

*coming in December 2000
from Silhouette Special Edition.*

*Turn the page for a sneak preview
of this exciting finale to the
Delacourt saga.*

"I want you to go," Tyler said gruffly. "No offense. It's getting late. Do you need a ride home? I can call a cab for you."

She shook her head. "My car's over by O'Reilly's. I can walk."

Tyler bit back an oath of pure frustration. "Not alone, not at this hour," he said. "I'll walk with you."

Her chin rose stubbornly. "It's a few blocks. I'll be perfectly safe."

"With me along, you will be," he agreed. "Got everything?"

She patted her purse. "Right here."

"Then let's go."

Outside, there was something about the heavy night air closing in around them that made Tyler feel as if they were still all alone. It was the kind of atmosphere that invited confidences. But instead, they walked in surprisingly companionable silence for a bit. Tyler hadn't realized Maddie could be so quiet for so long. Thrown off guard by it, he felt a sudden need to figure out what made this woman tick, to unravel the contradictions he'd sensed in her.

"Maddie what really brought you to my place tonight?" he probed.

She regarded him with surprise. "I told you, I was concerned when you didn't show up at O'Reilly's."

"You have to admit it's unusual to take such an interest in a virtual stranger."

Her gaze met his. "Not for me."

"Then you make a habit of riding to the rescue of people you barely know?" The thought bothered him for some reason he couldn't quite explain. On some purely masculine level, he wanted to be different, which was absurd when not five minutes ago he'd feared getting any more deeply involved with her.

"Only the ones with potential," she teased lightly.

"Potential?"

"Of becoming friends."

*Friends.* The word echoed in his head, annoying him irrationally. Had he been misreading the signals that badly?

"Can you believe how hot and muggy it is?" she said, stealing the chance for him to question the limitation she seemed to be placing on their relationship. "It feels like rain. Maybe that will cool things off."

Because she seemed so determined to move to an impersonal, innocuous topic, Tyler deliberately gave the conversation a provocative turn.

"Some people think there's something sexy about a sultry night like this." His gaze locked with hers. "The weather gets you all hot and bothered. You start ripping off clothes 'til you're down to almost nothing."

Maddie swallowed hard, but she didn't look away. "Sounds…" Her voice trailed off.

"Tempting?" he inquired, amused by her sudden breathlessness, relieved that he hadn't lost his touch, after all.

She blinked away the hint of yearning in her eyes, seemed to struggle to regain her composure. "Disgustingly sweaty," she said tartly. She turned away, then stopped, looking relieved. "Here's my car."

"Well, good night, then. Drive carefully."

"I always do."

For some reason he didn't entirely understand, he impulsively captured her chin in his hand and brushed a light kiss across her lush mouth. Maybe it was just so he could catch one more glimpse of that startled flaring of heat in her eyes. He was amply rewarded for his efforts. She stared at him in open-mouthed astonishment, but unfortunately that quick taste and her surprise didn't seem to be quite enough to satisfy him. Besides, her lips were soft as silk and sweet as sugar. What man could resist?

But even as he lowered his head to claim another kiss, she ducked away and slid into her car. The rejection might have stung if he hadn't noted the way her hands trembled ever so slightly before she clutched the steering wheel tightly.

"Good night," he said again, but the words were lost as she started the engine.

He watched her drive away. Then, instead of turning toward home, he headed for O'Reilly's, his throat suddenly parched. Rather than simplifying his life as he'd planned to tonight, he had a feeling he'd just made it a whole lot more complicated.

# LINDSAY McKENNA
## and Silhouette Special Edition present:

**MORGAN'S MERCENARIES**
**IV**
**MAVERICK HEARTS**

## These men were born for battle, but are they ready for love?

On sale in November 2000:
### A MAN ALONE
(Silhouette Special Edition® #1357)

Captain Thane Hamilton came home to Arizona
a wounded soldier unwilling to open his hard
heart to anyone. But once under the tender
loving care of beautiful nurse Paige Black,
this brooding warrior was filled with an
aching desire to live—and love—again.

## Only from
## Silhouette Special Edition!

*To my wife*

*I am the cute one!*

#1 *New York Times* bestselling author

# NORA ROBERTS

introduces the loyal and loving, tempestuous and
tantalizing Stanislaski family.

*Coming in November 2000:*

## The Stanislaski Brothers
### Mikhail and Alex

Their immigrant roots and warm, supportive home had
made Mikhail and Alex Stanislaski both strong and
passionate. And their charm makes them irresistible....

*In February 2001, watch for*
**THE STANISLASKI SISTERS:** *Natasha and Rachel*

*And a brand-new Stanislaski story from Silhouette Special Edition,*
**CONSIDERING KATE**

*Available at your favorite retail outlet.*

*Silhouette*®
*Where love comes alive*™